WELCOME TO TH

In your hands is a one-way ticket to the Old School.

It is a literary world that is shadowy and unknown. A fiction few today remember or have read.

This original "pulp fiction" represents an edgy and extreme chapter of black literary history. It is at once dangerous and deeply transgressive, gritty yet bold and experimental.

Your tour guide—a lost generation of black authors with street credentials born of hard times and tough luck.

Your destination—the charred remains of urban America. Places like Flatbush, Hell's Kitchen, South Philly, and most ominously, a federal warehouse for repeat drug addicts. But in the Old School, even suburban tree-lined streets can play host to violence, and a perfectly nice young man can become a twisted psychopath thanks to one small problem: his Mom.

It is an era whose time has come and gone. It begins as early as 1958 and leaves off about 1975. But this is not a sentimental journey. Get on board and you will visit a world inhabited by original players and hustlers . . . mack daddies and racketeers . . . police and thieves . . . cops on the take and girls on the make. Flawed little men with big dreams, bad guns, and no hope for redemption.

It is a world of the desperate and the deranged; the doomed and the damned; a world where the sun never shines.

You get the idea.

America wasn't ready for these hard-boiled dispatches when they first appeared, and they were lost to history. Reclaimed in the Old School they join Stax Records, 70s gangsta chic, and the blaxploitation flick as cultural artifacts to be embraced by a new generation.

These books deserve a second chance, and in the Old School, they get one. So get on board.

Marc Gerald and Samuel Blumenfeld, Editors
Old School Books

The Angry
Ones

OLD SCHOOL BOOKS

edited by Marc Gerald and Samuel Blumenfeld

The Scene CLARENCE COOPER, JR.

Portrait of a Young Man Drowning CHARLES PERRY

Corner Boy HERBERT SIMMONS

The Angry Ones JOHN A. WILLIAMS

The Angry Ones

JOHN A. WILLIAMS

Old School Books

W · W · Norton & Company
New York · London

Printed in the United States of America

The text of this book is composed in Sabon, with the display set in Stacatto 555 and Futura.
Composition by Crane Typesetting Service, Inc.
Manufacturing by Courier Companies, Inc.
Book design by Jack Meserole

Library of Congress Cataloging-in-Publication Data
Williams, John Alfred, 1925–
   [Angry ones]
   The angry ones / by John A. Williams.
      p. cm. — (Old school books)
   ISBN 0-393-31464-2 (pbk.)
    1. Afro-Americans—Fiction. I. Title. II. Series.
PS3573.I4495A82 1996
813'.54—dc20   95-45530

W. W. Norton & Company, Inc., 500 Fifth Avenue, New York, N.Y. 10110
http://web.wwnorton.com
W. W. Norton & Company Ltd., 10 Coptic Street, London WC1A 1PU

1 2 3 4 5 6 7 8 9 0

PREFACE TO 1974 EDITION

I finished *One for New York* in 1956. It was in the Fall. I felt like walking that day. It was raining, and I walked in the rain down Riverside Park from West 85th Street where I was then living to a track near 72nd Street. I used to run around that track to stay in shape, and because I had nothing else to do, except work on the novel. I was out of work, but I had finished a novel, my first. So I felt very good that day.

I am told that I wrote five versions of *One for New York*. They are in a collection somewhere. It seems that every time it was submitted, an editor would suggest changes, which I made. I do recall one rewrite. I was then living crosstown, on East 82nd Street. The possibility of acceptance loomed large, as definitely probable. I rewrote the book in 24 hours, straight through, on an extremely hot summer day and night, dressed in bathing trunks. It was not accepted after all. Options taken on it were dropped.

When Ace Books bought this novel as a paperback original, the editor changed the title to *The Angry Ones*. A better-selling title, he said. I mumbled agreement: I wanted the thing published. But I have never lived comfortably with the title, since it was not mine, but a stranger's. However, I was relieved to have the novel finally published.

That happened in January, 1960. It received one review in the Los Angeles *Times*. I had not expected much more. I could not begin to speculate on how much was read into the book because of its title. Ten years after its original publication, it was reissued in paper once more, under the same title. Now, 15 years after it was first published, and almost 20 years after writing the first version, I

am happy that it is now titled with my title, and I am grateful to
The Chatham Bookseller and Frank Deodene for that.

—JOHN A. WILLIAMS

New York City
Nov. 4, 1974

PREFACE TO 1996 EDITION

Thirty-five years after its initial publication the title of this novel
returns to its original: *The Angry Ones*. No doubt it is a selling
title. It is like "New" for the marketers. Everyone responds to
"new"; and few people fail to respond to "angry."

But, as I explained in the 1974 Preface, the title was not and is
not mine which, I like to think, called up deeper and more lasting
responses. It did this because there was no adjective in it that pur-
ported to explain or to make more saleable this book whose original
title was *One for New York*.

Teaneck, NJ
Sept. 22, 1995

JOHN A. WILLIAMS

JOHN A. WILLIAMS IS among the few writers in the Old School who have enjoyed an enduring and successful literary career, which is tribute to his drive, ambition, and talent.

Williams began writing while overseas in the Navy, though he didn't publish his first novel, *The Angry Ones* until he was 35. The book is loosely based on Williams's own frustrating experiences as the publicity director of New York's Comet Vanity Press. "What made me sit down and write the book in the first place," Williams said in a 1971 interview, "was that I didn't have anything else to do. It was a question of writing down some of the things that had happened to me. Seeing these situations in print made me rather determined never to forget them." Turned down by all of New York's most prestigious houses, Ace Books published the book as a paperback original in 1960 under the title *The Angry Ones*. As Williams explains in the preface to this edition, he had originally wanted to title the book *One for New York*.

Though this novel undeservedly sank like a stone, Williams's career was off and running. His second published work, *Night Song* helped make his reputation. His 1967 bestseller, *The Man Who Cried I Am* would solidify his place in the pantheon of postwar literary greats. A half-dozen works would follow—each drawing on themes of black pride and black sorrow in a hostile world. Hard-hitting and realistic, their enduring appeal owes as much to Williams's razor-sharp observations as they do to his immense gifts as a storyteller and literary craftsman.

After years in the academy, Williams recently retired, and is currently at work on a new novel. The reclamation of *The Angry Ones* in the Old School marks its return to print after a long and unfortunate hiatus.

The Angry
Ones

CHAPTER ONE

IT WAS HOT in Philadelphia where Andy had let me off. I had called a cab and now I stood waiting for it on the curb in front of the dirty little Christian Street "Y."

Talk about a helluva trip. Andy, another guy beaten by the Coast, was returning to Washington where he would go back to hacking, pimping and playing soprano sax in a combo. I'd met him in the Pigalle in Los Angeles—not so sunny L.A., as far as we were concerned. Andy used to sit in a corner when he wasn't playing; he sat and looked and smoked. We got along because I didn't have much to say either. Anyway, when he decided to make it back East, I was ready, especially since it was going to be an inexpensive trip.

I had gone west to visit my folks in Honolulu. They'd hit the numbers big after years of scuffling and saving, and had left the States. They never said why, but in my way I found out. When I left them I stopped in L.A. to visit my brother, Dave. He was four years younger than I. A good looking guy, he was, and his cheeks still had a youthful fat to them, so that they ran to dimples when he smiled. He had nice eyes, clear, warm and kind they looked sturdy and confident in that vibrant brown face. Dave stood a little under six feet, but he seemed smaller because he was a solid mass of muscle. You saw, when he walked, moving his shoulders easily, that he was trying to minimize the impression he gave of having great power. Sometimes, when I saw him coming up the walk where I shared his apartment, I could only think of him in comparison to the sad-faced kid left years back in a cart, and I would think in awe, *Damn*!

Dave went to school nights and worked days, making up for the time he'd lost in Korea. He was lucky; Grant, our brother, had not been so lucky. He was with the goddam Marines when they got their asses shot off, also in Korea.

Dave helped me through some rough spots. California, I found, could be as bad as Mississippi if you were black and looking for work in publicity—my field. At one point I took a job as a butler in Beverly Hills. I also collected bills, or tried to, and I got sucked in on a puff-sheet advertising racket, but fortunately only the publisher was picked up by the Fuzz. Things got even worse and I went more than 200 days without employment—I counted every damned one of them—and the day I did, I went for the Seconol, but I woke up anyway, hung as hell, but alive.

So I left Dave, the kid brother, feeling pretty ashamed of the times I'd beat his head in and sent him home when we were kids. And more than that feeling badly—too late of course—about not being with Dave more when we were all young. Dad, then, was out a lot of the time, making his money where and how he could. Grant got by on my father's affection for him and Dave was loved very much as the baby, but it was always me he wanted to be with.

You remember this when you stand on the same plateau, having arrived there only heaven knows how. And on that plateau you talk about jazz, women, the folks and The Problem. As I was saying good-bye to Dave, in the threatening heat of the night, I knew that I should have given more. But it was done; I could only be—as I was—sorry.

Andy and I left then, swung easily into the purple night beyond Pasadena, and before long edged into the packed heat of the desert. Just for kicks we got one of those canvas water bags to dangle from the radiator. They're like overseas campaign ribbons. When you see a car with one you know it has come a long, long way. We had a taste of bourbon with us; we nipped it as we tore along. I didn't drink too much of the stuff—it makes me feel like God when I'm driving. Two shifts and we hit Arizona in the morning. Later in the day it was Flagstaff, where they wouldn't serve us beer. We had to go across the tracks where the Indians and Negroes drank together in sullen silence. We left Flagstaff in a hurry.

Then we hit Tucumcari, almost without knowing it, and shot across the Panhandle in the middle of the night. It was hot and on either side of the car tall grasses trembled at the rush of hot metal. Occasionally a hulking jack rabbit, yellow eyes gleaming, darted across the road and vanished. The Ford hummed along on the black ribbons of road at eighty.

You remember a lot of things about a trip across America. You remember the sandstone rocks reared above red and brown plains, the twisted, fiercely shaped arroyos. You remember the way the Ford thrusts you back in your seat when you kick it in for passing, and you recall the squat and stately way the Cadillac moves even at 100 m.p.h. And the monstrous trucks you remember, sweeping from behind you with a rush and rattle, pulling around in and front, taillights growing dimmer, dimmer, and gone. And the Ozarks, they were beautiful.

Jefferson City was our first overnight stop and we put up at a loathsome, crawling Negro hotel, just at the foot of Lincoln University. We woke exhausted the next morning; we'd been fighting crawling and flying things all night.

Then we tried to get breakfast in a white restaurant, but they wouldn't serve us. We almost didn't leave Jefferson City because Andy, shouting something about a quarter of a pound of lead in his ass from the war, started over the counter and I had to pull him back. When we got to Wichita, we hunted until we found the Negro neighborhood and wound up at an elderly woman's home for fried chicken, bacon, eggs and a smattering of the Gospel according to St. John.

Finally, Andy and I grinned with relief across the table in a Massilon, Ohio, diner where we ate well for only the second time in two thousand miles of traveling. Then we were on the chain of thruways, Ohio and Pennsylvania. On the Pennsy, we kept pace with a car in which two girls sat nude. They were very friendly, but they didn't stop. They only waved and smiled and taunted us by slowing, if they got ahead, or speeding up if we caught them. We got off on the Philadelphia approaches and Andy dropped me at the "Y." He went on to Washington.

So I stood on the curb sweating. It was damned hot. The shower I'd taken fifteen minutes before wasn't going to be effective for long. The cab came and I lugged my stuff into it. We shot through Philly making it for the uptown bus station. The bus drove up as I got out of the cab and I ran inside to get a ticket. The clerk saw me and yelled over the loudspeaker to the driver, "One for New York—hold it!"

I ran back outside. The typewriter case came open as I climbed into the bus and I said a prayer: "God damn it!" I closed the case and stumbled up the aisle and took a seat. The bus started. After I caught my breath in the stifling heat, I hoisted the bag up on the rack and placed the typewriter in my lap. I opened my window, then looked around at the passengers.

There was a pleasant-faced salesman who looked ready to break into a pink, confident smile. A student, neat in his chinos and fresh shirt, was reading Beowulf in Anglo-Saxon; I could see this by the cover of his book. A stylishly dressed, middle-aged woman announced to her companion that she was tired of traveling by train and plane, and thought a bus trip would be nice for a change. A young woman tried to silence her loudly questioning child while a has-been sharpie wearing an outdated, wide-brimmed hat looked indulgently on. There were two soldiers and a sailor who got together and talked their particular language of barracks, leaves, liberties, sergeants, officers, women and ports of call. They drank while they talked.

A couple of carefully made up young women were figuring the best way to get from the 34th Street Station up to Times Square, and an expert driver, I gathered from his conversation, sat right behind the driver and talked about traffic and speed and the most gruesome accidents he'd seen on the road.

I shut out the sound of the voices and began to think of myself. One more hour and I'd be back in it, the peculiar American rat race, plus. I had that flash of fear which comes when I think of what I might be in another ten years. I wondered how many of the years gone by I'd wasted; I'd always been conscious of time and how fast it could go. It seemed I'd done everything I should have, but I was still running, feeling that oblique hunger for a thing I didn't even know.

I had had it all planned. My dreams, the things I'd been working for, were to pay off in another five years. They were not elaborate dreams; I'd have a job I liked, and I'd grow in it, have security in it and be able to do other things when I had time. It was in essence quite a simple dream. There are in America many people for whom work they desire is achieved as a matter of course. They don't have to dream about it. But I had some doubts my dreams would come off. Still, dreams can be either the best or worst things in the world to have. You're walking around dead if you don't dream.

I shifted in my seat. As the sports announcers say when the score is tied, "It's a new ball game," and it was. Starting time: twenty minutes. Twenty minutes—and if I didn't get a job in New York? I tried not to think of it. Don't think JOB, don't think it. Avoid it as an evil omen. *Say it*! I turned to look out the window. *Say it*! my mind shouted, JOB, J-O-B, Job. All right, Job. I'll get a job. Funny, other questions didn't bother me once I handled that one.

Other questions?

My family. My parents. There was a long line of us Hollands and Hills. If you wanted to, you could trace us from the Ivory Coast Baule to the Onondaga in upper New York. You could chart our course two ways from Africa—the early stage across the East, over the Aleutians, across the plains and mountains of the American West to New York. The late stage is easy—the sixteen-twenties, courtesy of the British, French, Portuguese, Danish or American slave ships to Jamestown or Charleston and down to Mississippi. And in all those years and through all that misery, adventure, life and death, I was the first to receive the skin with the college stamp on it. There are reasons, of course, why it had not happened in our family before. That is not my point. What is, is that it happened to me after generations of hoping and praying and working and groveling; it came to me for all of us. Yes, for even the first, whose captain, caught in the approaching winter storms, unceremoniously dumped his black cargo at Charlestown since he could not make New York port.

So my parents and each of those bearing a relationship to the family expected a great deal from me, for had we not been taught that education would make us free? And because of that belief, my parents, especially, tolerated what I thought they considered odd behavior: my drinking, which though moderate, was to them excessive because they didn't really drink; and the women, up until Grace and then after her.

I would cut my tongue off before I would tell them the sheepskins they wanted in their family were not worth a damn. Not for any of us; not for me, because it was only playing at a game allowing us to have it. But to give my parents due credit, I believe they were aware that conditions had changed—that getting a good slice of education these days in no way assured a life of comparative ease. But if they failed to believe what they had taught us—Grant, Dave, and myself—what *could* they believe? Like many of us, they clung to truth turned not to lie incarnate, but to untruth. I think too, in their slow, methodical reasoning, each clutched a bundle to the heart, for they had wanted so much for me, which was them, in a time when hoping had not a clear relationship to reality.

But they were for me one hundred per cent. In the long run of averages, I suppose, guys like me always have good people, and in the end it doesn't matter that they don't believe with you if they believe *in* you. You come home drunk or sullen or raging with your frustrations, ready to tear the place up, collapse in it, and somehow they know you're mixed up and they're kind to you at the right times, strong with you at the right times. They do almost everything right with you, even expressing a clumsy kind of faith for you when you've run all out of it. And with all this behind you, unspoken but as present as the oxygen you breath, you have, quite simply, another fardel to haul.

I had thought when they hit the numbers, packed and got the

hell out of the States, some of the pressure would be off, but it wasn't. They never said it, not once, but I knew I couldn't let them down nor myself. I remember the afternoon my father picked up the numbers money and came home. He never had much to say, but when he did, people moved. We were at dinner, the money in crisp new fifties neatly stacked beside his plate. We all looked at the money, of course, but said nothing. Finally he said to my mother, "Let's get the hell out of here."

It was the only time in my life I'd heard him curse. He didn't apologize; she said yes, and Grant, Dave and myself were busy peeking for the first time at his newly disclosed hatred of America.

So the ball was left with me, the Number One son. I couldn't let them down. I'd let them down once. I never told them. Even if I knew how, I wouldn't have. It was during the war, that crazy, useless war in Italy where the brass had sent a couple of million men as a compromise to Churchill's "Soft Underbelly of Europe" invasion plan. I'd always wanted to be as big a man as my father. He'd been in the 369th in France during World War I. He got a chestful of medals from the French and a very bad time from old Uncle Sam.

I was on the line Christmas Day, 1944, with the 92nd Division or what passed for it. You know the 92nd—it was one of the two all-Negro combat divisions in the war. We had had some things on the way up and I was beginning to feel like a real infantryman, but on Christmas Day, when the Germans came out of those holes, ripped off the sky and dropped it, hot, smoking and screaming at us, then launched a heavy breakthrough, I bugged out. I wasn't alone, but I bugged, and that was something I couldn't tell the folks; there aren't any cowards in our family.

The heat in the bus made me sleepy and I dozed off. I came back to life as the Empire State Building hove into view above Jersey marshland. We drove into the tunnel and when we came up we were in the sweltering city and my twenty minutes were up.

Getting off the bus, I walked to the 34th Street side of the station and got a cab. We drove to a hotel on 42nd Street. When we got there, a young bellboy hopped over to take my bag. It almost pulled his shoulder blades out. He gave me a sheepish grin and went for a hand cart. Up in the room, I tipped him and mumbled something about a drink. He told me I had to wear a tie in the lounge, so I slipped one on and went down.

The Yankees were playing the White Sox at the Stadium, and everyone in the room, their faces uplifted as wilting white mums seeking sun, watched the television set above the bar. It was a stupid scene, that, but I had nothing better to do and I joined them, sipping the drink I'd ordered. Yogi Berra belted one into the stands and, ridding himself of his surprised look, began to jog around the bases as the bar filled with Mel Allen's "It's in there! Now, how about *that*!"

The images on the screen grew bright, then fuzzy. I was tired, and the drink and the trip had all but put me away. I went upstairs, took a shower, opened the windows and lay down. I started to read a magazine, but I put it down for a moment remembering.

Once, while Grace and I were engaged, we were in New York for a week end, and now—crazy! I could fantasy her in the room, smiling her lovely smile, sitting with her legs crossed or moving like shadow-clouds across a sun-filled summer field. I sat up suddenly and shoved the bed away from its corner. I got down on my hands and knees and lighted a match so I could see. It was there, scratched in with a nail file, *Steve and Grace.*

Very gently I placed the bed back. I climbed upon it with a certain tenderness. Then I looked at the phone. For a long, long time I thought about calling Grant's widow because way down, somewhere, I was still in love with her. But I didn't call. I told myself I wouldn't be worth a damn for my appointment at NBC in the morning, the one I'd made on the Coast, if I didn't get some sleep.

CHAPTER TWO

I AWOKE rested. I dashed down to the drugstore and got a cheap, quick breakfast. I walked slowly into the street, on my way to NBC. New York has a way, when you catch it just right, of doing things to you, and I felt then that the city was doing something to me, for I began to admire its people, its buildings, its busyness. It was relatively cool. A haze softened the stark outlines of the midtown buildings and I had a great feeling of, not hope, but confidence.

By the time I got past the Plaza, I had worked up a good sweat from the walk. I paused before I got on the elevator and wiped my forehead, then I stepped into the car. The personnel office was filled with handsome people, male and female. They sat awaiting their turns with one of the personnel officers or they filled out application forms. They were probably complete strangers to one another, but in their manner and dress they appeared to have been cast from the same actor-starting-at-the-bottom mold. Not quite the bottom, for the days of Gregory Peck at the Music Hall and Gordon McCrae in the Radio City usher corps were all but past. The people in the personnel office would begin as assistants of some sort and work up to NBC television. A few would become stars and later they would be talked about.

"Yes?" the receptionist asked. She impressed you with her alert manner.

"My name's Steve Hill. I have a ten o'clock appointment with Mr. Giddings."

She checked her book, then looked up brightly. "Oh, yes, Mr. Hill. From Hollywood, aren't you?"

"No, Los Angeles."

"But our Hollywood office set up the appointment?"

"Yes," I said, thinking about the interviews I'd had at Hollywood and Vine, where NBC was. Nearly everyone in the room had turned to look at me when she said, "Hollywood." How square can you get? Hollywood is an alleyway; it is less than McDougal Street, but its name covered all scratches. Hollywood—you don't argue about what it's come to mean in our time.

"Mr. Hill," the receptionist said apologetically, "would you mind filling out this application? Mr. Giddings will see you as soon as you've completed it."

When I finished the application, she directed me into the inner quarters of Mr. Giddings' assistant. He was young. He gave me a big, wide smile and the great big hand. He went over my application, saying, "Hmmm, hmmm, hmmm," and nodding approvingly. After reading it he picked up his phone. I thought to myself, What a fool you are to worry about a job. See, you've got one already! When he hung up, he said to me, "Miss Gail would like to see you. She's in charge of the correspondent section. Our publicity people come from that department. It's a steppingstone, you see?" He smiled. "Now," he continued, "I can't promise that there's an opening, but you can get the interview anyway. Right?"

"Right," I answered like a damned dummy. Then I went downstairs and talked to Miss Gail. The salary was small. It surprised me, but I would have taken the job had there been one, but there wasn't. I returned to Mr. Giddings' assistant. My face must have mirrored what I felt.

"There should be something breaking in Miss Gail's department before long," he said. "Someone's always getting promoted. You'll like working for NBC. Our policy is to hire people on their ability— we don't care what the color of a man's skin is. And we don't," he said breathlessly, "blow our own horn about our nondiscriminatory policy, like CBS." He smiled.

I smiled back to let him know I was impressed.

I wasn't. I didn't give a damn who crowed or who didn't crow over the fact that they hired Negroes indiscriminately as long as I got a job. I left Mr. Giddings' assistant's office with these words thundering in my ears: "I think you'd be a tremendous asset to NBC. I look forward to seeing you around here soon."

So I got out of there, went downstairs and killed the rest of the morning over coffee. I knew New York was dead after 11:30. The guy you want to see gets in at 9:30, 9:45. He breaks for coffee about 10:15. From then until 11:30 he's busy, more or less, until noon or one o'clock when he goes for lunch, which could string out for a couple of hours. You don't get a good interview in the afternoon; it's got to be morning or you're dead. I drank coffee.

I called Linton Mason, a friend from college and the old days, and got invited to dinner that night. The call finished, I had nothing to do. I needed a haircut, though, and I didn't want to go all the way uptown where all the Negro barbers were. Too hot. I found a small shop near the UN. The barber was white.

"Say, doc," I said as I went into the shop, "think you can cut my hair?"

He looked at it, then at me. "Maybe I not do so good a job, but I give a goddam good try," he said, and I thought, New York, I love you. While I was in the chair, I kept thinking, Dad, you ought to be here. The haircut was not bad. I went back to the hotel and got ready for dinner at Lint's.

Lint and I had been in college together. He married Bobbie there. It was the time of the crush of veterans; of Dixieland's revival; of the assonance blending with a dissonance in modern jazz with Parker, Stitt, Monk, Garner, Dizzy, Sassy; it was the time when Henry Wallace, borne on the shoulders of youth, scared the hell out of both the Republicans and the Democrats. It was the season of impatience: Where were the better things?

They were not to come. The Peeksill Riots made us know it. The trials at Nuremberg made us know it. Whatever had been in the air—and there *had* been something—was gone. We had been a generation like the Jazz Age, and like it, we had been overwhelmed by the dead weight of national inertia. We would be named years later, laughed at, pitied and perhaps studied in a section of freshman surveys of American literature.

But in the days of college, Lint's work and mine were termed "searching"; poetry and prose not too good, but "searching." Now, as I rang the bell to his apartment, the time past was almost like a scene remembered from a movie.

He hadn't changed much. A little bigger in the gut, but the same boyish exuberance. Lint was medium-tall, had sandy hair, a pug nose and bright brown eyes which seemed too far apart. He had a certain absent-minded charm about him. Lint seemed always apologetic for being white, Protestant and American. I liked him and I never doubted he liked me. He was rather bookish and could sometimes affect a pedantic manner, but all told, he was quite fine.

"Well," he said, as if I'd been late for cocktails, "where the hell you been?"

"Nowhere, really," I said. I flopped on the couch and studied him. Balding. A little flabby. Wrinkles here and there.

Bobbie came out, her hair as coppery as I remembered.

"Steve!" she shouted. "Lint told me you were in town. How good to see you!" We embraced.

I chuckled. Bobbie Mason was a real armful of woman. She was thin, but taut. You couldn't be around her for any length of time without wondering when she would explode. "Honey, how you doin'?"

"Oh, fine," she said, kissing me in that quick was she had.

"Hon," Lint said, "fix us a drink, will you?"

Bobbie spun out of my arms. "Why don't *you* fix them?"

They stared at one another.

"Me," Lint said. "Why me?"

"Oh, crap!" Bobbie said. She glared at Lint and went stomping into the kitchen. Lint looked at me and shrugged. We sat down in silence.

"What do you want, Steve?" Bobbie called.

"Anything," I answered. I turned to Lint. "How was Italy?"

His eyes shone. "Fabulous," he said intensely, the way you speak of a beautiful girl you remember well. "You should have been there. Steve, I wrote two novels, twenty-three stories and fragments of a hundred poems. I haven't sold a thing yet, but Italy is beautiful."

And I, of course, told him about Honolulu, Los Angeles and Vegas, but it didn't sound like Italy and Lint waited for me to be through so he could tell me more. I let him tell me.

At dinner the cloud which had blown up so quickly went away. I watched them. They had always been extremely happy; I envied

24

them. They didn't have kids because they were busy carving out careers. Lint was an editor at McGraw-Hill and Bobbie was a promising actress. Lint was my age, had about the same training, same desire to write. But he was making it rather easily; I was not. I could not find it in my heart to wish them ill because they were white, but I suppose sometime in the future, if things get bad enough and I have to go to a head-shrinker, he'll probably tell me I really hated the hell out of them. I don't think so. Envy, certainly, but not hate. Matter of fact, had I had anything to do with the choices of brothers, I would have had a difficult time choosing between Lint and Dave. For real.

After dinner we talked about the people who'd been in our gang in college. The thin, Jesus-looking English major who had come out of the army at forty and breezed right through for his degrees. He was teaching in the South. Then there was the beetle-browed editor of the school paper who, married and the father of four children, took off with the richest, prettiest coed on the campus. We talked about the sweetheart of Sigma Chi, who went with a Negro basketball player and who was asked to resign from her sorority. And so the evening ran on. Our short conversation about Bart brought me up short—there was still the problem of a job.

Lint said, "You remember Bart, don't you?"

I wasn't sure, but I said, "Yeah, I guess so."

"Sure you do. He was at that last big party we had before you took off. He had a beard then. The artist . . ."

"Yeah, yeah, I remember."

"Well," Lint said chuckling fiendishly, "guess what he's doing now, him and his goddam art?"

"What—ad agency?"

"Yes!"

I know I looked surprised. Bart had been rather purist about his art—said he would never work in an agency. I felt a little sorry for him. Anyway, talking about Bart brought Lint to asking about my job.

"None yet," I said.

"You can always bunk here until you get straightened out."

"Sure," said Bobbie warmly.

"Something will turn up." I laughed to hide my embarrassment. "I've only been in town a day. Just keep your eyes open for me, will you?"

"Sure," they agreed.

At the door Lint said, "You got back just in time, Steve. Party season. Good ones coming up." He slapped me on the shoulder, then I left.

The subway was steaming. The heat drained my energy and when I got off the car I could barely climb the stairs. I went along the street, plodding, pushing along, head down. I couldn't think of anything but the heat. Near the library, I thought I saw a familiar figure, but I paid no special attention to it. I was wondering if I shouldn't take a cab for the balance of the distance to the hotel.

"Goddam, ol' Stephen Hill." The voice was deep, unruffled and familiar. I turned.

Obediah—Obie Robertson, a classmate Lint and I hadn't talked about, stood there, a smile on his face. Obie and I had crossed trails frequently around the country, but I hadn't seen him now in about three years.

"Obie," I said.

"Man, it's good to see you," he said.

"Thanks."

"Where you making it to? Living here?"

"Hotel," I said. "Just got in. I'll probably make it here. Say, I just had dinner with Lint Mason.

"Crazy," Obie said. "Everything. Flipped when I saw you. I heard you were on the Coast, man."

"Yeah, starving to death."

"Hell. You can do that here. But all the guys have been sounding me on how great the Coast is."

I snorted, then I said, "Walk with me up to the hotel."

"All right."

Obie was a big, good-looking guy—the big personality without being the big pain in the ass. He'd finished college with honors, but the journalism school couldn't place him because he was a Negro. He'd worked for most of the Negro weeklies and was now editor of *World of the Black*, a big picture book patterned after *Ebony*.

"Job?" he asked as we walked.

"Man," I said with some heat, "I just got here."

"Sure, sure," he said.

We walked in silence a few paces, then he said, "Look, you need some money, let me know. I can spare some."

"Thanks," I said. I felt good because of his offer. As we entered the hotel I said, "I don't suppose you have any openings."

"No. Sure could use some help though. The book looks like it's getting ready to fold."

"Yeah?"

He nodded.

I had never been in his office, of course, but that didn't stop me from imagining the way it probably was—unmatched furniture, poorly lighted, dull floors, ten-year-old typewriters and a living doll for a receptionist who did nothing but talk pretty into the phone, smile and wave her fine legs at visitors.

"How's Lint?" Obie asked suddenly.

"All right. He's making it."

"Sure is," Obie said with a rueful smile. He looked at me and I returned the smile. We understood, but neither of us would speak what we knew so well.

We stopped in the lounge for a drink and exchanged news of Negro reporters around the country. "Tompkins just moved up at *Jet*—assistant managing editor."

"I ran into Collins in L.A.," I said. "He was moving to Vegas to start a paper there."

"Davis took a job as PR man at Provident," Obie said.

"Sewell went to Ghana, I hear. No?"

"Yeah, he cut out. Said he'd had it."

We were silent a while and I knew that Obie, like me, was thinking of all the time spent in journalism schools and how little of it could be used when you worked on a Negro newspaper, and how rough it was—how damned nearly impossible—to get something on a daily paper.

"You married, man?" Obie asked.

"On what?" I scoffed.

Obie laughed. "*All* broads want that security—they don't care what you think you can do, if no one's going to let you do it. They want you to fit in, anywhere, as long's there's a pay day." Obie chuckled, more to himself than to me. "I haven't made it either, Steve."

"We're getting damned old, too," I sighed. "This chasing broads doesn't seem to get it the way it used to."

"I know," Obie said with a smile.

I thought about it as I sipped my drink. I said, "You know, Obie, I was ten years old when my old man was thirty." I thought about it again. "I should have a couple of kids right now."

Obie nodded soberly. "I was twelve when my old man was thirty. He must think my dick got shot off in the war. He looks at me awfully funny sometimes."

I damned near spilled my drink laughing. Obie. Obie Robertson—how good for him to be around. He saw how he broke me up and he smiled, pleased. He took out a pencil and some paper.

"This is my stuff. Give me a call tomorrow. I'll see if I can't pry something loose. Don't count on it though." He gave me the paper and stood up. "Look, man. Don't be an ass, you need bread, let me know. There's no theater between you and me."

"I know."

"Well, act like it." He pounded me on the shoulder. "Glad you're in town, man."

He went out then. I sat. I guessed I must have smiled, for I was thinking, *Bread*, the staff of life. As Obie and I used it, it was the staff of life all right, only it was *money*.

I went to the lobby and got a *Times* and rummaged through the employment section up in my room. I marked some jobs, then hauled out the typewriter to do up some letters. I inserted resumés with the letters into envelopes and dropped them into the chute in the hall.

Back in the room again, I toyed with the idea of calling Grace. I decided against it, but having had the thought, I couldn't get rid of it, so just before I went to bed I called.

It was good to hear her after I worked past her kids who were still up. I wanted to tell her what room I was in and in what hotel, but I was so intent on catching any shadings in her voice I forgot to. She sounded very good. She wanted to know when I was coming to see them. As soon as I got settled, I told her. The night was better when I hung up than it had been the night before.

CHAPTER THREE

I WENT "home" the next morning, home to Harlem, and made the rounds of the papers, the same papers I'd applied to weeks before my graduation from college. I hadn't received a single answer then. But I was back. A sympathetic editor offered a deal on a space rate basis. I turned it down. I'd done space rate copy before, and starved. It probably wasn't the editor's fault, but his paper was known among writers for paying slowly. I was in no position to write reams of copy for pennies and wait six months to collect them.

We chatted a while on the continuing problems of the Negro press, still a weapon rather than a medium. We talked about the lack of newspapermen on the papers. Advertising personnel, at least for the present, were a shade more practical because they brought in the money to pay for the paper, the writers, the printers and distributors.

I couldn't sell Cadillacs if they went for a dime each, I told him. He agreed I didn't have it—the quick, the dash, the glib required of the sales representative to sell the Negro market through his newspaper.

He had heard that Obie's magazine was on the verge of folding. He'd been trying to talk his publisher into putting up money for Obie's salary, but the publisher wasn't having any. The editor and I went out and he bought a beer for me. We stood talking then, on the street, with the black, brown and beige crowds surging around us. He told me as I left, "In heart, don't ever get too far away from Harlem. The stuff of history is right here."

I thought he would laugh when he said it, but he didn't.

On the way downtown I thought of what Obie and I had talked about a couple of years before, that as opportunities for Negroes appeared on the surface to be getting better, they would at the same time become subtly worse for some segments. The gains made in the blue-collar areas would be balanced by heightened barriers in the white-collar fields, and would be toughest in the professional fields stressing public contact.

I had been told that New York City's employment agencies were the worst offenders against the state's law against discrimination. But I had to try them—I couldn't pass up any angle.

In the first agency, tacked on the wall, was a big State Commission Against Discrimination poster. It didn't give me any confidence. I filled out an application and handed it to a receptionist. She asked me to have a chair. Some other applicants came in. We exchanged glances. There were no expressions on their faces, but I got the idea that this agency was supposed to be a pretty exclusive little club—they had looked at me just a fraction of a second too long. I know that look pretty well. Finally, I got inside with an interviewer. His name was Thomas.

"Don't have a thing right now, Mr. Hill. Why don't I keep your application and give you a ring—say in two, three days?"

My next interviewer, in another agency down the street, seemed ill at ease. He kept looking around, as if to discover who was responsible for letting me in. He tried to rush me through in a hurry.

I asked what his rush was. It boiled down to his having nothing for me. I went to two other agencies that day, and I had the feeling, as I headed for the hotel, that I would get nothing from an agency.

Obie had called, so I called him back.

"How you makin' it?" he asked.

"Nothin'."

"It'll break. Be cool."

"I'm not worried," I lied.

"We'll get together in a couple of days," Obie said. "I want you to meet Gloria."

"All right."

I hung up, showered and went out to eat. I felt like nothing, so after dinner I showered again and smoked myself to sleep.

The next morning I dashed down to the state employment office on lower Fifth, then rushed back uptown to hit more agencies. I drew a blank all the way around. After lunch I called Bob Graham, another classmate. His mother answered. Bob, she said, was in Argentina running an advertising agency. I was surprised. She said he was doing quite well. She asked me to call again after I got settled.

I wasn't feeling so well when I hung up. Bob and I had taken a lot of courses together in college. He was a dummy from way back. I was the boy who supplied the answers for him. I remembered how I used to feel his bony knee digging into my thigh—his reaction to the instructor's asking *him* a question. Down I'd go—I liked him—tieing my shoe laces, whispering up brilliant things for him to say while he parrotted them.

I headed back to the hotel then, too discouraged to think about anything except not spending another miserable night alone. I wondered what to fill it with.

It came to me in the shower. I could fill it with Kit Higgins, a tall, willowy girl with a nice shape and not too dull a mind. Kit was a "writer's freak"—she associated only with writers, dated them, slept with them. I called her and we arranged to get together for dinner. Kit had been in college with us, and had been in NAACP, the SDA and all the other progressive things.

Halfway through dinner I was sorry I had called her. It was not that she still wasn't attractive and wonderfully put together. I just tired of her harsh, high-pitched voice that seemed to erase the memories of the good times we'd had before. She was still concerned with the inane things that had fascinated her years before—what happened on her job, her love affairs, the new writers to watch for. I could no longer be, or pretend to be, concerned with them. When she asked about my world, I refused her entrance as though it was shabby and unkempt. Then, as people will do when seeking comfortable ground, we began talking about the people we had known at school. She wanted to know if Lint had become a successful writer and I said not yet. Kit brought up Don Zubinsky.

Don had been in a couple of Shakespeare courses with Obie and me. Between classes, when Obie and I would stand in the hall, watching coeds and smoking, Don would often drop over and talked about the course, reading much into it that sounded like a class war. He wanted us to join his organization. That was the gist of his every conversation with us.

"I know what you guys have to go through," he said one day. "Believe me, I know. I go through the same thing. I'm Jewish."

Obie looked at me, then at Don and said, "It's not the same thing. You can change your name. It wouldn't work, though, for us. So it's not what I'd call the same."

"All right," Don admitted, his face a little red. "It's different, but you've got to fight and we're here to help you." He clenched a big, meaty fist. Obie looked at it, looked at me. I looked at it, then at Obie. It was quite a fist.

"What did you have in mind?" Obie asked cheerfully.

"Come around Saturday night to our place. There'll be a party and lots of girls." He smiled and rolled his eyes. I became angry, but Obie smiled back coolly. I'm sure we interpreted the same thing from Don's grin. "You'll find out for yourself what we can do," he finished.

When Don left, Obie said, "What time shall I call for you Saturday?"

"Don't call me. I don't want any part of that outfit." I was steaming. "Dangling broads as bait to get us in."

"Well, man," Obie said, "I'm not interested in the party, but I do want to dig how great their free love is."

We laughed. Obie made the girls all right, and managed to avoid the politics; but Zubinsky, Kit was telling me as we drank coffee, had been tagged as a third-string Communist leader.

"I'll be damned."

"It was in the papers about six months ago."

"You remember Obie Robertson, don't you? We had some classes with Don."

"Oh, yes!" Kit said with sparkling eyes. "He was so smart! He must be worth a lot of money by now. I haven't run across any of his stories though . . ."

I sometimes forgot Obie was a writer too.

We lapsed into silence with our second coffee. The evening wasn't as gay as I'd expected—not like the night I'd left New York. We'd had a big, wild party then, with Lint and Bobbie and the hundred other people who always show up at parties and who are all so pleasant with their bellies filled with liquor. Things change.

It was time for me to do something. I didn't want to be alone again and I didn't really want to be with Kit. I didn't know who I wanted to be with—I just didn't want to be alone.

"Let's go back to the hotel," I said. I don't think I'd have been angry if she'd said no, but she didn't.

She rose from the chair. "All right," she said.

But halfway to the hotel I stopped. "Can I take a rain check?" I asked.

She stopped, too, and looked at me carefully. "You're having," she said, "one of those writing moods and nothing can keep you away from your typewriter. Am I right?"

"You're right," I said.

I put her on the subway and that was the last I saw of Kit. I felt somewhat sad when the train pulled out because Kit was the sort of girl who in her own way gave a lot to writers; to how many I'll never know. She was a one-woman phalanx against loneliness.

Up in the room, the cars cascading down Second Avenue, their tops reflecting the harsh lights of the *Daily News* Building, my worries returned and I could not sleep.

So when Lint called I was wide awake.

"I got a lead for you, man," he said.

I waited.

"It's vanity publishing, but it could turn out all right."

"What the hell's vanity publishing?"

"You know. Where people pay to have their books published."

"Oh," I said. "Yeah, I know."

"I'll have more for you tomorrow."

"All right. Thanks."

"Forget it."

"Night."

"Night."

CHAPTER FOUR

I HAD BEEN trying not to think about it—getting out of the hotel and looking for a place. It would have been nice to have got hold of a job first, and avoid having the two problems to handle at once. But I had to get out. That horrible imbalance—outgo but no income—was beginning to become pronounced. And so, one morning not long after I had talked to Lint—"tomorrow" didn't necessarily mean the next day with us—I got a *Times* and raced through it looking for a place. I called a spot down in the West 20's, then went to see it.

Big, ugly garages gaped silently in the mid-morning shadows.

Kids played stickball in the streets. Curtains hung listlessly in the heat. The place I went to see had a crayoned sign which read *Vacancy*. I rang the doorbell. A woman answered.

"Yeah?" she said. There was a frown on her face.

"Could I see the place you're renting?"

"Oh! I can't rent it."

"Why?"

"I—uh—lady's coming back this afternoon to rent it. It's already taken, you see?" She smiled then, after she had got her lie out without stumbling too much over it.

"Yeah, I see."

There were other places in other neighborhoods for me that day. Sometimes the superintendents or their wives didn't answer, although I could see them lurking behind the shades if their quarters were just off the door. Other times the places had been rented, but the super had forgotten to take the sign down. It was late in the afternoon when I got back to the hotel and looked through the paper again.

"Hello," a woman's voice answered when I called the first place on my new list.

"I'm interested in the place you have for rent."

"Fine. Come right over. The address is—"

"I'm colored," I cut her off, wearily.

There was a pause.

"Well, I wouldn't mind it at all," she said. "It's the neighbors. They wouldn't like it. And I have to please the neighbors."

I got angry, hot.

"Do you own the place?"

"Well—" she said, then angrily: "Yes! I own it and I will not rent to you!" She hung up.

A jovial-sounding woman, older than the first answered my second call. "You have a place for rent?" I asked.

"Yes, yes, a very nice place."

"I'd like to come and see it."

She gave me the address. "It has two big rooms, bath, shower and tub, closets, and it opens on the front."

"That's very nice," I said. "Do you have Negroes living in your building?"

She laughed scornfully. "Negroes? Naw! No Negroes, no Puerto Ricans. I run a nice place. I"—her voice came back into the void I'd left—"are *you* colored?"

"Yes," I said. "Yes, I am."

"Well, I'm so sorry. I cannot rent it to you." She hung up quickly.

I waited a long minute before I turned to the next name.

I called the final place on my list. I got a real estate broker's office. The girl who answered said the place was nice, lots of room and all.

"You have vacancies *now*?" I asked, looking at the ad.

"Oh, yes, lots of them." She gave me the address of the apartment.

"Very good," I said. "I don't suppose it makes any difference if I'm colored?"

"No. Oh, no," she said after hesitating for a split second. "You just go right over there and if there are any vacancies the super will show them to you."

I hung up. I wanted to laugh, then I wanted to cry, but I did neither. I just hung up and sat looking at the phone like an ass.

It rang.

"Boy, is your line busy," Lint said.

"Yeah," I said.

"I got the poop on this place. It's Rocket—are you taking this down?"

I whipped out a pencil and began writing on a piece of paper. "Yes," I said, "go on."

When he finished, I looked at my watch. "I'll call now. Maybe I can catch them and set up something for tomorrow."

When Lint hung up, I dialed the number he had given me and asked for a Mr. Culver, who was, thank God, still there. We arranged an appointment for the following afternoon. I would have time to walk the streets in search of a place tomorrow morning, and if I was lucky, I'd have a job tomorrow afternoon. I went to bed that night feeling much better than I had in days.

In the morning I took a bus up to the West 80's and, getting off, I walked from Riverside Drive to Central Park West, up one street, down another. New York can change abruptly from one block to the next, from quiet residential streets with baby trees to teeming, littered ones filled with shouting, lounging people. On the nice streets I had little luck. On the bad streets—Well, who wants to live on a bad street? I finally came to a stop before a new sign on a not-too-bad-looking building between Columbus and Amsterdam. A pleasant-looking man was dawdling over new furniture in the freshly painted lobby.

"I'm looking for a place," I announced.

"A kitchenette?"

"I don't know. Let me see what you have."

He had only one place left and it was five flights up. It was as large as some bathrooms I've seen, half as small as some others, and the rent was seventeen a week. One window opened on the scarred brick facing of the building next door. I took the kitchenette with great reluctance; it was still cheaper than the hotel. I got my receipt and told the man I'd be back the following day. He said all right.

I couldn't help but comment, "It's hard for a Negro to find a place to live if it isn't in Harlem." It was more for myself than for him.

He shrugged. "I rent to everybody. And it's all right here. I would live here myself."

"I bet you would," I said.

I left then. It was getting late and I had to get downtown for my appointment. The streets were jammed with Negroes and Puerto Ricans. Most of the stores had Spanish names. Kids squeezed through among the adults, begged for nickels and dimes and cursed you if you didn't give them anything. Rouged women, some sullen, some artificially vivacious, stood in doorways and on the curbs. Men, resting their backs against parked cars, eyed them, eyed you— anything that moved in the street. On Broadway the black and tan tide lessened. Elderly people with wrinkled, pasty faces and thick-lensed glasses sat wrapped in blankets in the sun, dying quietly, easily, unaware or unconcerned with the floods of people lapping quietly behind them, just a block or two away.

I headed downtown to Rocket. The office was located in that craggy mass of office buildings which rests on 42nd Street between Fifth and Sixth. I was shown immediately to an effeminate-looking man who introduced himself as Roland Culver. He was well-dressed. His suit of dark-blue mohair was beautifully cut; his striped tie was a soft blue and white, and was finely tied with just a hint of a crease below the knot. His pin-collar shirt was white on white. His gray hair was combed in a slight curve back over his head; it glistened. His lips were thin, and matched perfectly the thin bridge of his nose. His blue eyes were set deep but alertly in their sockets and sparkled soft and feminine. A small diamond shone on his finger. His hand, when I shook it, was long, soft and dry. I studied him more as we sat down and he began to examine my folio.

He nodded as he looked at the samples. "Good, good." He looked at me with a brilliant smile. "I have one question, Stephen. Has most of your work been among Negroes, for Negro papers and magazines?"

"No."

I told him my background in detail. He watched me with a little smile. He was satisfied. The salary was not the best, but it was a start. It was a job.

He explained to me what co-operative publishing was; he didn't use the term, "vanity." It sounded fair enough, challenging enough. I've always been a sort of sucker for challenges, and Roland Culver must have spotted this right away, or perhaps it was something else he saw or knew.

But I had a job and it was in my field.

I explained that I was checking out of my hotel and Culver said it would be all right for me to start a couple of days later. I went swinging out of Rocket and checked out of the hotel into my new place. I called Lint and Obie to let them know about the job. They were elated, especially Obie. So was I, of course.

But my elation was cut through the next day by an incident which reminded me that there was little place for happiness—just yet.

My first day in the new place I came to know the strange scents of cooking—the strongly spiced Puerto Rican foods, the thick smell of hot starches, the cabbages. I could hear the conversations of the people next door or the toilet flushing down the hall. When I ate, I pulled the blinds down so the little kids across the alley could not hang out their windows and watch me. When I sat down to write that first morning, I was conscious that the sounds of my typewriter were alien in that place. Yes, I am sure the landlord would live here, in my room, any room in the building, on the street for that matter. He would live here, sure, with the heat screaming silently in from the asphalt streets and the tarred rooftops. He would live here, an animal in a hole, except when away from it; he would live here and worry about whether or not the toilet seat down the hall would be clean if he had to go, and if it wasn't, how best to clean it. Sure, he would sit and watch the kids in the next building swing from the window sills or crouch beneath his own window and listen to the sounds of the husband and wife across the way making love, while shouting for the kids to stay out of the room. Yes, I'm certain he would live here and pay his seventeen or twenty or twenty-three promptly and without grumbling every week.

I was still thinking about it when I put away some dishes I'd got at the five-and-dime. Some man on the floor below was shouting to a woman in the next building. The woman next door had been sneezing—had hay fever or something, because she had been at it all afternoon.

"Aw, shut up!" the woman shouted in answer to the man.

"Bitch! I said stop all that goddam noise!" the man shouted again. The way his voice carried, I guessed he was leaning out the window.

"Why don't you lay down, you drunk bastard?" the woman screamed between sneezes.

"You just stop all that goddam noise," the man said.

The woman must have leaned out her window. Her voice was suddenly loud. "Listen—Oh! He fell!"

I heard the sound. It was like beef being thrown on a chopping block. I went to the window and looked down. The man, clothed only in shorts, lay on his back. Blood was beginning to flow from under him. An ugly splotch of grayish yellow began to form near his head. He seemed out or dead—I couldn't tell. I got my camera and took two shots before the heads poked out of the window below. People began to fill the little alley between the buildings. They stared at the man, whispered. Occasionally there was a hysterical laugh. The man on the ground tried to turn over. He screamed and jerked and lay still.

"For God's sake," a woman said, "get a doctor."

"Is he hurt?" the voices asked. "Is he dead?"

"What happened?"

Two cops came—one white, one Negro. The white cop seemed apologetic, the Negro cop was gruff and sharp. Some garbage was flung from the rooftop into the alley, striking the cops and everyone else below. In a flash the colored cop had his pistol out, pointing it skyward toward the unblinking little Puerto Rican girl who had thrown the stuff down.

"What the hell's the matter up there? Can't you see there's a man hurt down here?"

The crowd grew silent. It watched the pistol, the cop, the little girl, who moved slowly away from the edge of the roof. I drew in from the window and dressed so I could run to a phone—they hadn't installed them in my building yet—and call the *News*. I heard they paid for good pictures and I could use the bills. I got to a drugstore and called. I asked for the desk and was shifted from one department to another until I got the man who handled the spot pictures. I told him what I had.

"Did you take the shots in mid-air?"

"No," I said. "A minute after he hit the ground."

"How many stories?"

"Five."

"Is he dead?"

"Not sure. Looks pretty bad."

"Is he a colored man?"

"What?"

"Is he a colored man?"

40

"Yes," I said. "Why?"

"We can't use them."

"What do you mean?"

"Can't use 'em. Thanks for calling."

He hung up.

This, I thought over a cup of coffee, is the New York I bragged about in L.A.? I sipped the coffee. I didn't want to think about it, but it kept coming back. "Is he a colored man? Is he a colored man?" Since when has a colored man's death been less final to him than the death of a white man?

There were crowds in front of the building when I got back. Ambulance doors were opened. They came out with him on the stretcher. He was all covered, from head to foot.

Good-bye, Sam, I thought.

CHAPTER FIVE

*T*HE NEXT DAY, my first on the new job, I had to concentrate on what was being done, so I could not think too much about the day before. There was much to do. We did a lot of canned reviews and I jumped right in on that. There were, as time went on, manuscript reports to get done, advertising and promotional copy to write. It became my job, also, to set up promotion campaigns for each of the authors to be published that year. One thing surprised me, later, was that most of the manuscripts I'd given poor reports on eventually showed up in production. I figured Roland Culver knew the business better than I.

But it was good to be working. At lunch I burst into the sun-filled streets and mingled with the crowd, feeling once again that I had some purpose in being. I seldom took a full lunch hour, even when I read the paper—I always rushed back to get into the work. It was nice. You feel better when the end is blocked from sight by things to do, things you like to do.

But being without this—without a job, without something to do when you want to do something—is the worst thing in the world that can happen to you. In the morning, while millions of people are eating, dressing, rushing to work, where are you? Dragging around the house, pretending you're glad you don't have to go to work that day; but the pretense leaves in a few days and you begin wondering what the hell is the matter with you, you can't get a job. A slow, clinging fear works into your system and stays there no matter how hard you try to chase it away. So when you are offered a job, any job which has the semblance of a salary you color it, make it a nice job, a little less perhaps than what you really wanted, but not bad after all.

So now I had me a job, and to me it looked good.

I gave Rocket Publishing everything I had. Sarah, Roland Culver's secretary, was astonished, and that astonishment gave me pause, for why should she have been astonished had she not in the first place not believed me capable? And if this was so, why, *why* was I hired?

The pause, however, was momentary. In the days that followed, I was not unconscious of the fact that I was the only male in the office besides Rollie. He was Rollie to me now, as he was to everyone except Sarah; she called him Roland. I will not say that in time I even forgot I was Negro. I didn't. But it was not the first time I found myself the only Negro in an office. It was not a good feeling nor a bad one; merely curious. But the setup here, though, was different from what I'd known.

Ours was something of an interracial office. Anne was a little Japanese Catholic. She'd come to New York from San Francisco only a year ago and her primary concern was becoming sophisticated. She disliked Japanese men and went out only with whites. She was very nice-looking with her finely carved, calm face. She was a little on the stocky side, with not too much breast. At first I was quite sure she didn't like me; if she didn't like Japanese men, would she like colored men? Later, though, she came to me to discuss her sex life—women in New York are always discussing their sex lives whether they have them or not. Anne had a fixation—she thought I knew all there was to know about sex. I had never discussed my sex life in the office, so it was odd that she chose to discuss herself with me. Eventually I got around to asking her why she disliked me, but the denial was too quick, too eloquent. In other words, she was lying through her teeth. But we managed to get along in the office.

Harriet was a middle-aged, slim woman with an arm crippled by polio. She lived in New Jersey with an elderly aunt. She was tremendously aggressive, I guess because of the arm. She joked a lot about men, and always she told me how clever I was, how charming I was, how well I dressed. She had a habit of looking at my pants as if she were lost in thought. It made me uncomfortable. I got into the practice of standing behind my desk so she could not flick her eyes up and down.

She kept asking me to lunch with her until I gave in one day and we went downstairs. The lunch became uncomfortable when she began asking questions about my girl friends. I didn't feel like discussing my love life with her, especially when I sensed something not quite wholesome behind her questions. I hurried through lunch with the excuse that I had some things to take care of before I returned to work, and I left her. Harriet was an editor. I supposed she would find it difficult to find work just anywhere. But along with my sympathies I retained the conviction that she had a problem or two.

I guess I liked Leah best. She had dark hair and green eyes, and a nice figure too. She was a quiet girl who worked very hard. Her typewriter, when she was on it, sounded like a machine gun. She was lots of fun and I never had an uneasy moment with her. She shared her miserably black coffee with me, even when I didn't want it. "Puts hair on your chest, Steve." We lunched together often or walked around, shopping. Leah became like a sister. When the pressure was on, we shrieked and shouted at each other like dogs, and when it was over we kissed and made up. Leah was really a swell woman.

Sarah had a way with Rollie. She was about forty and had the eyes of a small animal, soft, brown, quick. Her expressions were always changing; they fascinated you, but it was her eyes you had to watch. I first noticed them the day Rollie interviewed me. She had smiled prettily then, but her eyes had been searching. Later, I discovered she found what she had sought.

Sarah was a totally unexciting woman. She was built with big breasts, stiff hips and thin, little legs. Her hair was gray and cut in gray strings which always seemed to catch in her glasses. She talked fast—sometimes spewing saliva on you if you weren't careful to stand an extra foot away from her—and she walked fast, as if she might miss something if she didn't. Sarah appeared compelled to create situations where she had to employ whispering shrewdness.

I saw little of Rollie; he came in late and left early. Often he had midday conferences out of the office, but when he was in, it seemed that Sarah acted as a shield, keeping herself between him and us. But I fitted in well. I knew it and they knew it. I was happy and felt liked and needed. I did some free-lance work and I got back to writing. It was all a very wonderful feeling and I began to think more and more about Grace.

We grew up in the same town upstate. I think I have been in love with her since the first time I saw her in our church in a black velvet coat and muff with white trimmings. She didn't, at the time, live with the rest of us; her parents were something or other in one of the big houses up beyond the park and maybe this kept them away from our neighborhood until the father died. Then they moved down with us and Grace's mother joined our church. I guess it went pretty hard for them, since they weren't used to the hard lives we lived, and more than once I saw sadness in Grace's eyes at church affairs. Eventually, though, Grace and her mother came to be well-liked.

Grace and I became engaged—that's what we told each other it was—on a church picnic, and I recall that she kissed me in the basement when we came back to the city. And once, around Christmas time, when the local movie houses showed an hour of cartoons, Grace and I sat together and I slipped a five-cent ring on her finger. We were quite carried away.

We liked everything about living as we were growing up—the summers splashed with the blue lakes and green hills; the autumns with the ochres, reds, browns and greens, and the scents that went with them. We loved plowing through the snow in ski parkas and ski boots to a movie after church on Sunday or to a party or a dance where, when we danced to Glenn Miller, everything seemed just *so right*. And in the spring we'd borrow bikes and ride into the country and occasionally I'd have enough money to get horses and we'd select a couple of nags and jog through the deep, beautiful valleys which surrounded our town.

Grace was a little tall. Her color was a soft new-leather brown and she had upslanting, dancing eyes and a beautiful mouth I never tired of kissing. I learned her body completely. I knew its smells, its curves and hardnesses; I knew how she would respond and when; I knew what each gasp or sigh meant. Even our silences meant a thing I could understand. I never doubted that we would marry.

Grace's mother became bedridden and I began to see less and less of Grace. She had to go to school and she had to work and she had to study and care for her mother. I suppose that was the time the fierce desire for security was born in her. And it grew. It became a monster which consumed the love we had for each other as if it had never existed. But the war came, and for a time, through our letters and on my two furloughs, we seemed to have recaptured the things that meant so much to us. But after the war I saw that what she had done was but a war-time measure.

My brother Grant was the same age as Grace, and a dumbell could see that he was in love with her, but she was my girl—that, I never doubted. We became engaged—this time it was the real thing—as I began college. I could tell she was not pleased with the field I had chosen, but she said nothing then. It was only after college and after a couple of years of grubbing around that she said she wanted security and I was not going to have it in publicity. She

4 5

wanted me to become a social worker and get a civil service job. I refused, not because I didn't love her, but because I did so much. She left me. You know how people get to call you and your girl's name with a certain rhythm? Like Tom and Betty, Paul and Susan, and so on? It'd been Steve and Grace for so long that for years after, people were always stumbling over her name when they talked to me.

Anyhow, Grant was around after we broke off. He was steady, unimaginative and still very much in love with Grace. He was a skilled machinist and made good money. Hell, he was making good money when most of the plants in the city were only giving out janitorial jobs to Negro applicants. Grant had had his share of the Hill drive. Once he set his mind to a thing, that was it. They married, though Grace discouraged him for a long time, I suppose out of kindness for me. They moved, after awhile to Albany, where Grant got a better job. They had the things—a home, a car, insurance, all that goes into what it takes to be secure in our time.

I visited them when Grace was pregnant with Teddy. We sat on the porch, just the two of us against the background of autumn. Grant was working. She was so lovely with that child in her, and her eyes were so lustrous and warm. I was quite shaken and I was in love with her more than ever then, and the only thing that saved me was knowing that in spite of everything, she still loved me.

Then Grant went away to Korea and he stayed there in one of those frozen valleys. I felt sorry for the bastard—to have died so young and to have left Grace and the kids, Teddy and Frankie. It was his death that made me feel so guilty about still loving Grace.

CHAPTER SIX

SINCE I was now making a little money, I decided to look around for another place. The one I had was so small, if you fell you'd be lucky to hit the floor; you had to hit a wall or something. I began moseying up and down the streets after work. The big apartment buildings were closed to me, I knew, but I was hoping to just fall into a place, I guess. I suppose I should have known better. Looking for an apartment you can afford is a full-time job and it is a Herculean labor if you happen to be Negro. Then, one week end, on the spur of the moment, because the weather was going to be nice, late summer, I decided to go up to Albany and visit Grace, and maybe go to the place where we grew up.

I had never thought much of Albany as a town. It had nothing to do with the experiences some of my friends had had there when they went into the navy—Albany was the navy induction center where they separated the black from the white and sent them off to war. No, it wasn't that. It's a town that's laid out all over the hills. It's pretty until you get into it, like almost everywhere else.

You take the New York Central up, shooting out of the underground at 98th Street. You rise heavily above the streets looking into the windows of the uptown slums; they rise on either side of you. Out of the windows people hang, if it is warm, and their faces are all the same, dull, flat, sullen or sad, and their eyes follow the train hungrily and you know they wish they were on it too. Then, to the right, Yankee Stadium shoulders itself into the sky, and you think of the Bombers, the baseball machine, and you wonder how little fun is left in baseball, and how little fun in anything. A minute later the Polo Grounds, with its big orange signs, is there, on the left. Then you are bending against the screeching rails as the train rounds the curve behind Baker Field, and you straighten out and rush through suburbs, up past the Thruway Bridge, Bannerman's Castle, the Point and the Rip Van Winkle Bridge. If you are sitting with a west view at sundown, the sun shatters streaks over the Cat-skills and you know that although she has flounced her beauty too many times to be counted, and for a long, long time in a great unapplauding silence, she is at that time of day as breathless and beautiful as a spanking new ingénue.

Not that I was thinking of these things when I arrived.

Feeling foolish and happy and a bit nervous, I called Grace from the station, hopped into a cab and went over. She stood tall and relaxed in the door, the season all around her. She was wearing shorts which showed her long, well-formed legs. Her eyes danced like the rays of the sun kissing the tips of tiny waves on a quiet lake. Her hair was tousled and fell carelessly over her forehead. Her mouth widened into a smile of welcome and she moved toward me.

The kids, Frankie and Teddy, smiled tentatively beside her. You could tell they were not used to being still so long. They looked like both Grace and Grant. I mean the features were there. They had Grant's square, rocklike face and Grace's delicate eyes and her long body.

"Hello, baby," I said.

"Steve, hello." Her voice had a curious quality, like the ringing of bells heard deep within a woods, telling you the direction of home.

After so many years and so many things, it was good being there. I hugged her, smelled the smell of her. I felt the curves of her body as she leaned against me and I saw, through half-closed eyes, the wonderful lines of her neck. I released her, fighting hard to keep my breath measured. The kids had been watching us with deep, still eyes that must have, in their brightness, caught everything. They retreated a step or two backwards.

"Hello, Teddy. Hello, Frankie," I said.

They looked at Grace and she nodded. "Hi," they said, starting to grin.

"I brought you something," I said.

They grinned again, but this time at each other, as though they had made a wager and this was the payoff. They jammed their hands in their pockets, but took them out again when I gave them the gifts.

"Run along and open them," Grace said.

When they had disappeared inside, Grace said, "What have you brought for me?"

You know, it was one of those two-way questions.

I said, "You're not a kid."

"But didn't you bring something for me?" She gave me a curious smile.

"Don't be so damned clever," I said. Then: "You look *so* good, Grace."

"And you." She took my arm. "Let's go inside." When we were in the living room, cool drinks in hand, she asked, "How are the chicks treating you in New York?"

I didn't answer right away. I had noticed that Grant's picture was nowhere to be seen. When I turned to ask what she'd said, a little smile was playing about her lips and her eyes danced.

"Sad," I said. "They're treating me very sadly."

She nodded, but it was exaggeration; she didn't believe me.

"How are you making it?" I asked.

She gave a little laugh and pointed to the kids who were just then galloping back into the room. Then I was lost in accepting their thanks—kissing them and getting kissed in return, holding their hand and listening to each of them in turn and together. I didn't get another good look at Grace until after dinner. I put the kids to bed then. Frankie had forgot the Lord's Prayer and I had to say it for him three times.

"Why don't you know the Lord's Prayer, man?" I asked. I wasn't upset that he didn't know it. I mean, what the hell.

"Teddy says them for both of us," he said, smiling across at his brother.

Teddy jumped up. "Do you know why?"

"No, why?"

"Because I'm Superman!"

They cracked up. No lie, these guys belonged in my family. I stood near their door ready to snap out the light. Teddy said, in a tone unlike any I'd heard him use during the day, "Uncle Steve?"

"What is it, Teddy?"

"Uncle Steve," he rushed on, "do you like our mother? Are you in love with our mother?"

"Yeah, are ya?" Frankie said.

"What makes you ask that?"

Teddy crept close to me and his smile was filled with the mischief and tenderness kids can sometimes have. "You do, don'cha?"

"I like your mother very much," I said. I snapped out the light.

"You going to marry her?" Frankie shouted in the darkness. He laughed and Teddy joined him. Then they said good night and I knew they were through having fun at my expense, at least for that moment.

I closed the door and went to the kitchen to help Grace finish the dishes. I kissed her on the back of the neck, the way I used to when we rode in the valley and stood looking out over a green ridge. She stopped moving her hands in the water and turned to look at me, but I'd moved off to a rack for a cloth.

She filled in the awkward silence. "Mom still in love with Hawaii?"

"Yeah, she and the old man. Having a real bit out there."

"Got a letter from Dave last week," she said. "When's he going to get married?"

"Soon, I guess. He's got a real nice little doll."

"He's a very wonderful guy," she said.

"Yes, he is." I was thinking of the morning after the Seconol when he kept asking me, "What's the matter, champ?" I didn't tell him that I'd got halfway to hell and come back. After a long silence I asked Grace, "What's with you, hon?"

"Nothing. Just working and raising the boys." There was a hint of bitterness in her voice.

"I thought maybe you'd be thinking about getting married again," I said, with the biggest goddam lump in my throat.

"Sure, I'd like to." She was washing the dishes very rapidly and I thought, Well, there's no one else.

50

"What are you waiting for?"

"I don't know."

"Teddy and Frankie just tried to get us married off . . ."

She looked at me in the queerest way. She smoothed her dishcloth over a rack and lighted a cigarette. She exhaled the smoke coolly and looked at me. "Yes?" was all she said.

I tried to smile and it fitted awkwardly upon my face. I tried to get a cigarette that refused to come out of the pack. All the time she just looked at me and it was as if I had no tongue at all.

We left the kitchen and went inside to watch television. About midnight she made up the couch for me. I sat in the blue glare of the TV set alone while she got ready for bed.

"Grace!" I called impulsively.

She shot through the door of her room, her diaphanous robe billowing behind her. I met her halfway across the room and felt her body drive against mine. We kissed and afterwards she said, "Ooohh." And it was like I always remembered it, that sound, the soft echoes of it.

"Grace! Oh, Grace!" I said over and over again. It was all I could say. We sat on the couch and we whispered and clutched one another and Grace sniffled and cried softly and I might have, too, I don't know. It was dark and I know my face was wet—her tears or mine, I don't know. We sat there and remembered. Man, how we remembered.

The smell of horses against the mint and pine of the valleys; the smell of fresh, running water; the sense of a complete and good world as we sat beside an empty lake in the fall with no one around for miles.

Finally she said, "It's always been you, Steve. You know that."

Man, I tell you WHOO Eeeeee! At that second there was nothing impossible—I could do anything. And I said, "I know, I know, I know." We were off and running. We'd get married, have a home for the kids and have more kids and it would be just as we'd always wanted it.

"But first," I said, eagerly, "I want to get a good job, baby, a really good job."

"I thought you had one."

Then I had to tell her about Rocket and my pay. She said I could leave and take something in civil service—that we would have security because of Grant's untouched insurance money.

Something went out of it then, and we were back in a living room with the television set going.

"Grace," I said. "I've been through too much to give it up. This marriage has to be on my terms."

"Your terms haven't changed and they're just as frail as ever," she said.

"And yours," I said, "haven't changed."

All that remained the same was my love for her and, damn it, I knew she still loved me and maybe it was the thing so stubborn in me that she loved the most. Anyway, she left me. Much later I turned off the set and lay listening to it ticking into coolness. I smoked and listened to the noises of the night and I didn't get to sleep until day began to come. I woke late and was headed for the john when the phone rang. It was Grace calling from downtown where she was shopping with the kids. She asked, "Are you all right?"

"Yeah," I answered. I wanted to communicate my gruffness to her. I did.

She asked, "What's the matter?"

"Grace, I think I'll take a run to the old homestead. I'll stop for a while on the way back."

She was silent a moment, then said, "Sunday night?"

"Yes."

"Oh, Steve, we counted on your staying the whole week end."

"We?"

"I."

"I'm sorry."

"Steve." Reproach was in her voice.

"I said I was sorry."

"All right, then. I'll look for you Sunday night."

"Good-bye."

"Steve?"

"What, Grace?"

"Please stop on your way back."

"I said I would."

"Steve?"

"Yeah."

"Oh," she said in exasperation. "I wanted to say something very important, but I can't talk when you're like this."

"S'long, baby."

The train hurtles along the Mohawk. To the north the Adirondacks begin to swell, at first gentle mounds of green and brown, then hills covered with trees and on into great garnet-speckled mountains. Along the river the wide and green fields flash by, still luxuriating in the richness brought thousands of years ago by the glaciers. The river narrows into a marsh which spreads southward and is abruptly gone. The land, now solid, is cluttered with kettles and gouges, boulders and baby drumlins. Old Revolutionary War memorial shafts point toward the skies like outmoded rockets on their launching pads, and you can almost see the Continentals, drummer boy in front, blue-clad, ragged marching idiotically over those open fields toward the British redcoats. Industries, the dead and the living, announce themselves on brick and wooden buildings as the train flattens out, streams past them.

Overhead the sky goes from blue to yellow and to a darker blue again, and the shapes of things beautiful during the day hulk forlornly in the dark. Across the way cars, their light beams needles in the night, rush without end on the Thruway, and the stars calmly pin up the night so that the moon may behold what is below.

I have been home many times and I always sought that special thing I didn't know, but felt I lost there. I became both glad and afraid when the train jerks, pulls, presses downward against the tracks, begins to slow. And when it finally stops, and the steps go down, steel clanking in the air, I want to run where, I don't know. Just to fly with the wind rushing in my ears and with my eyes running water from the whistling air.

Things began to settle, though, once I got outside the station. I hurried to the little club where no whites are allowed except cops. Before, I went to the club every Friday and Saturday night when the other bars had closed. The place hadn't changed. It even smelled the same. I had a couple of quick ones for bracing, then I surveyed the place for a girl—Somebody's Daughter.

I didn't see her but I did see that the records in this place hadn't changed either. Someone played "Nancy" and I began to think of my old buddy, Rowe. We'd been in the army together. When we came out we must have set something of a record for Saturnalias— every night. When we were kids, he won an amateur contest. He wouldn't perform before the audience, so the judges allowed him to go offstage and sing, unseen. "Nancy" made me think of him.

I remembered the times we double-dated. We would usually wind up in some thin-walled hotel, and I could always hear him telling his girl, "Thank you, dollin'." He was so damned polite. I asked him why and he said, "I'm just grateful, and when I'm grateful, I say, 'Thank you, dollin'."

He could really sing "Nancy." In the early mornings on the way home he would do it. It always seemed springtime then. We would amble along the deserted streets, each of us with an armful of woman to hold for a few hours, and Rowe would sing. God, how he would sing!

I thought of Rowe as I leaned on the bar. I didn't know where he was; they all leave, if they can, because in that place the force which is evil prepares one early for life of a sort. And if they leave it means that they have gone to seek other than evil. Good for us in childhood and even in adulthood was simply to resist evil since that was the active force, good being passive. Few people taught us that good was a positive thing. They said, "This is bad and that is bad and that also is bad. Resist them."

The good things somehow just happened. Like Sundays. Sunday really began with Saturday night when the bathroom was busy hours on end, what with the bathing and hairdressing. My father sipped beer he'd made and plucked the chickens he'd bought Saturday afternoon in the Italian section. My mother straightened her hair, but this would not be completed until Sunday morning, after which she'd brush Dave's hair by the hour, it seemed, while my father would tend to his favorite, Grant. Saturday then would melt into Sunday, and while my father went over Grant's hair again, my mother turned on the RCA radio which said inside, *Equipped for television attachment*, and got the program "Wings Over Jordan," only she said, "Jerdan."

How that choir poured out of that little radio! Really poured out, singing, "Go Down, Moses," filling the whole house. And when my father joined, singing the bass, the place quivered. Then he got into his gray suit and went off to church. He sang in the choir and had to be there early. My mother swished around, pulling and tucking at Dave, combing her hair and singing in a determined off-key voice until she was radiant and ready for church, managing things somehow so that dinner would be ready when we got home. When we left the house, piles and piles of browned chicken, hordes of stringbeans and biscuits, yams and salads lay ready for our return.

In church we always marched down the middle aisle to the front pew. I had to go along, although I would have preferred the rear pew. I could see my father in the choir, dressed like the others in a black robe. I could single out his voice, rumbling along beneath the others, providing a deep, soft bass for the other voices to tread on. I suffered through the services and only became gay again when the choir started to file down the center aisle. I looked up eagerly, waiting for the long lines of black-robed people to pass so I could catch my father's eye when he winked at us. I had to smile back— I couldn't wink without twisting my face. Then we went home for dinner.

"Steve Hill! Haven't seen you since the night you and Grace broke up, right in this club!"

I turned. It was, of course, Somebody's Daughter, but what she had just said finished me for the night. I couldn't be interested in anything now. I said hello and offered her a drink, which she accepted. Time seemed to have had whims with her. In some respects she looked very old and worn, but in others quite young and fresh.

She chattered on. "I suppose you're all over her by now, though," she said.

"Sure," I said. "Sure."

"You look well," she said.

"So do you," I said.

We had another drink and I said good-bye. I went out to wander around the empty streets, looking for what, I just didn't know. But I looked anyway. It was cool outside, and walking along I could almost hear Rowe singing "Nancy," hear the click of high-heeled shoes and the voices of women.

I looked and I looked. There was the spot where our pup had been mashed to death by a car; there was the stretch of road I'd helped with by laying cement in the summer. My initials were still there. But these were none of the things I was looking for, and I caught the train at daybreak. As soon as I got it I thought of Rowe again. It was sort of funny, the way we drifted apart. He decided not to go to school. That was what had done it. There had been a time when we'd meet in the streets and he'd want to talk about pussy. I was more interested in Pope and Proust. Then we didn't even bother to stop. We just waved at each other and passed on.

I didn't stop in Albany. I was undecided until the very last moment, but I didn't. I went to sleep and didn't awake until the train was slithering its way underground to Grand Central. I called Grace as soon as I got home. I tried to explain, but it's difficult when you don't know what it is you're trying to say.

The next day, Monday, would be a work day. I could bury myself in that.

CHAPTER SEVEN

THE FIRST thing I did the next afternoon was to go in and ask Rollie for the raise Rocket had promised me after the first couple of months. Rollie was very affable. He pulled out a bottle of martinis and we had a little drink. He told me he was pleased with my work, that I was a definite asset to the company, but—Of course there had to be a "but."

They couldn't give me the raise just yet, it seemed. Rocket was a relatively new company, it was just getting on its feet. It would not grow too much, Rollie said, and he himself planned to move on after he got the business going well. His spot would be mine, since I'd already proved myself capable. In fact, Rollie said, I had more on the ball than he—I could not only talk with the authors, I could handle promotion and distribution and publicity as well.

Rollie sold me on the challenge. I left the office almost happy with the peanuts Rocket was paying. On the way back to my own desk I was already noting the changes I'd make when I took over for Rollie. Old Rollie Culver. He was a fascinating person to know. He had a great deal of charm. He was the sort of guy who could do five things at once and do all of them charmingly. He seemed to charm the hell out of Sarah. I heard once that they went together, but it seemed odd to me, what with Rollie's being a flit and all, though I wasn't sure. But then perhaps Sarah was one of those women who prefer that type to another for her own special reason. They got along very well in the office. If you saw one, within seconds you'd see the other. They were inseparable.

It was Rollie's job to talk with authors. He was more interested in the prospective ones than in the ones already published. When an author, prospective or not, walked in and met Rollie's dazzling smile—which carried in it just a hint of wistfulness (Gee, I wish I could write)—the contract, if there was one involved, was generally as good as signed. Authors already published and dissatisfied with the sales of their books were, as a rule, mollified in a face-to-face session with Rollie. Securing contracts was Rollie's forte. The rest of us were what the *Times* ads called "self-starters"—we worked largely without supervision. This left Rollie with plenty of time to think up new ways to secure book contracts.

There was a lot about Rocket that I didn't know until later. One of the things was that a company like Rocket was primarily geared for printing. The contracts secured by Rollie through direct mail, personal contact and magazine advertising represented total profit to the printers, who set type for the books when the presses were empty. The books were supposed to be ready on a set schedule, but they seldom were, because printing was always coming in. Editorial work, publicity and promotion were basically decorations. There was no sales department.

Working with that secret portion of human nature which balks at frustration and obscurity, companies like Rocket do very well; they need the frustrated ones, though. First there is an outfit like Rocket. Then there is the writer or a person who writes. A friend says it is good. Other friends say it is good. Very often the writer is far past middle age. And, too, perhaps the community has displayed irritating disregard for the genius in its midst. For these people it is not enough to have lived and died and enriched the ground. This simple scheme escapes them. They must do something then, and, too often unequipped, they write. And wanting to do this, they are compelled to show it to friends and others who are kind. Having been compelled to show it, they are then compelled to publish it, and when the announcement is made that the manuscript has gone to New York, it must not return unpublished. And in New York, Rocket and similar companies sit and wait and sometimes are alerted by cheap literary agents who are paid for their referrals.

But I didn't know this until later.

I had to take on several part-time people to get my work out. Sarah screamed, but Rollie calmed her down. Going home nights, shoving and cursing in the crowds, I reflected again how good it was to be working. In the evenings I spent a lot of time looking for a new place. I finally found one which was only twice as big as the first, but it had a private bathroom. For the time being, I was happy to have found it. The rent, however, would have put me into an East Side midtown building, if I could have got in. I spent one night carrying my belongings from the old place. A funny thing happened that night.

I had got hold of a couple of very good marijuana cigarettes. I had one of them on me when I started moving my things—the place was only two blocks away, so I was carrying my stuff. Out of seven million people in New York, at least two million must carry stuff in bags every day, but the cop on the corner had to stop me. Me, with a roach in my pocket. He asked if the stuff was mine and I told him it was. He made me identify myself, which I did. He let me go then, but I was so shaken I flushed the cigarette down the toilet.

I would have forgotten the whole bit, but the following Saturday I was walking with Bobbie Mason to the store. Lint had stayed home to watch a football game on TV.

A police car cruised up and stopped beside us. A fat cop leaned out the window and hollered, "Hey!" We turned and the cop motioned to Bobbie. She walked over, tugging at her shorts. The cop gave me a dirty look. To Bobbie he said, "Those shorts aren't long enough, lady."

"What do you mean?" she snapped. "I've been wearing these shorts all summer."

"I can't help that. They're too short. You'd better get off the street."

I had walked to the car with Bobbie. I could see that the cop was waiting for me to say something so he could pour me inside and cart me off. I said nothing. I did even better than that—I walked back to the curb and waited for Bobbie.

"To hell with them," she said when she joined me. The cop watched us.

"Better go home," I said. "I'll pick up the stuff for you."

"To hell with the stuff." We stood there a moment on the curb. She looked at me. "You think it was the shorts?"

"No," I said.

"Those lousy bastards."

I walked her back home thinking how much I disliked cops.

"C'mon upstairs," Bobbie said as we stood in front of her place. "I'll fix a drink for you and Lint and you can watch the game."

We started upstairs. She whispered, "Don't tell Lint."

"Why not?"

"He told me not to wear the shorts."

"So? He ought to know what happens when his wife walks around the corner with a friend, oughtn't he?"

"Steve, this week things are going all right. I don't want to give him anything to bellow about. Christ, it's bad enough just listening to him."

"Oh," I said.

"Yes," she said.

"I didn't know."

"Not many people do."

"Planning anything?"

She had been walking ahead of me. Now she stopped and turned. "Nothing," she said. "Nothing at all."

We proceeded upstairs. When we walked in, Lint peered at us from his chair. He looked first at Bobbie, then at me. "Where are the groceries?" he asked. "You've been gone a long time." He rose; his mouth was laughing beneath lowered eyelids. He patted Bobbie on the rump. "You haven't been to Steve's place, have you? I remember Steve. Fast worker."

"Don't be silly," Bobbie said. She began to walk out of the room as though it would be beneath her to even answer her husband, but she said, "I didn't feel well all of a sudden. Steve brought me home."

Lint turned from me; he had been staring very hard. He became all at once extremely solicitous about Bobbie. I sat down while he made her go to bed. I looked at the television program, but my mind was on Lint. He was a man who was lost outside the center of the stage. He thrust himself upon anyone, anywhere and at anytime. He did this most with Bobbie, of course, breaking into her stories, recalling in a loud voice the punch lines she'd goofed, and so on. His were not opinions so much as judgments.

"You know I was only kidding, man," he said when he came back into the room.

"I know," I said.

"Poor kid," Lint said, settling himself. "She's been working too hard, trying out for things. Rough grind."

"Yeah," I said. I wondered why he thought Bobbie and I had been together in bed. Was Bobbie shacking up—or was it that he just didn't trust me? Lint had changed. I felt he was going through a rough time and I could not be angry with him. Besides, I was indebted to him for getting me the job at Rocket. As far as Bobbie was concerned, no one with a sense of touch or sight would have kicked her out of bed, but I had never thought about her that way, with me. I'm sure the thought never came to her either. My good friends, the Masons, had themselves a problem.

"There's a party tonight," Lint said. "Should be a good one."

A good party was something we had in common. According to Lint's definition, a good party was where everyone got crocked and where women outnumbered men four to one.

The party that night was the first of a series. You became alcohol-stunned and electric. Your laughter became whiskey-sparked and your lusts rose whining in the early morning. You watched Lint and Bobbie, if they were there, as you listened or danced to Dixieland, the Cool, Calypso, Mambo, Cha-Cha-Cha. You listened to Odetta and Bill Broonzy, the songs of the Lincoln Brigade. You talked of Pete Seeger and Leadbelly, and you got way down with the blues Sinatra sometimes wails the hell out of. And then morning came, so soon or was it finally? And those men who hadn't brought women or those women who hadn't men to bring them, surveyed the rooms of the party a final time, if they hadn't picked someone up or been picked up, and then went home to wait for the next party the following week end.

I was to be glad whenever Monday came, I thought, but when it would come there would be, until Thursday, the fight against the ennui a job you know well brings you. On Thursday, you begin preparing, tapering off for the week end. Late, very late on Sunday, depending on how you felt, you wanted very much to get to work on Monday. If this was not your wish, it could only be that Monday came too quickly.

CHAPTER EIGHT

*T*HINGS began crashing in after that first wild week end. My part-time help didn't come in and I discovered that Sarah had let them go, with Rollie's permission. "We just couldn't afford it, Steve," Rollie said. He'd come into my office to ask me to do a presentation for a prospective author who wanted to know what Rocket would do to promote his book if he signed a contract.

"Well, how about the raise?" I asked Rollie. "The money you were paying the part-time people could go to me. I'll have to do a lot of extra work to stay caught up."

"Steve, Steve, believe me. I want you to get more money. God, you're the best thing that's happened to Rocket. You deserve it. But I can't do it. I swung the part-time people for you, but the folks downtown figured we didn't need additional help. I told them, 'Look, Steve says he needs help, he must need it. He wouldn't say it for nothing. I want Steve to get the help he needs to do that job right.' Look," he said, gesturing helplessly, "give me a few weeks more on this. I'll see what I can do. All right?"

I nodded. What else was there for me to do?

"By the way," Rollie said, "I've got a couple of tickets to *Three-penny Opera*. Would you like to go with me? For tomorrow."

His eyes licked across mine quickly.

"No," I said. Then, thinking that too curt, I said. "Have to see my girl tomorrow."

"All right," he said, again very affably. But then and there I wondered if I would ever get my raise. What in the hell would I have to do to get it?

"Now about this presentation," Rollie said. "It's got to be good, Steve."

"How big is it?"

"Eight thousand."

"Eight thousand?"

Rollie nodded. "It's a massive thing. It'll be by far the largest manuscript Rocket ever handled. It'll be a feather in your cap and mine if we land it—mostly yours."

"Is it any good?" I asked. I was learning.

"Same old stuff. The author is a farmer from Mississippi. In some of his letters he sounds very prosperous, but who's kidding who, Steve? Who in Mississippi is prosperous? The state has the lowest income per capita of any state in the union. I guess he can get the money, though. I'll offer him time payments."

"What's it about?"

Rollie, on his way out, turned and smiled. He held himself in the stiff way women do when they are showing you a new dress. "The usual crud," he said with his dazzling smile.

When he was gone, I went over the file he'd left on my desk. When I was finished I had a good idea of what Crispus—Hadrian Crispus—wanted. I did the presentation, which Rollie liked very much.

"We'll get this," he said. "It's very good, Steve. God, I wish I could get that money for you right now."

Rollie was at his best with Crispus. He sent a letter to him every other day with a gentle warning that he might miss the chance of big Christmas sales if he didn't sign the contract soon. He even called Crispus a couple of times. The conversation, from Rollie's end, could have been laughable if so much had not been at stake— that is, so much of Crispus' money. The last phone conversation went like this:

"Yes, Mr. Crispus. Yes, that's right. This is Mr. Culver from *New York* calling again. Yes. Fine, and you? Good. Very good, sir. I hope you've come to some decision, sir. We're holding our presses right now, waiting for you." Big pause. "Mr. Crispus, you don't have to worry about it. It's a good book, a wonderful book, and you'll be doing the world a great injustice if you don't let it see the light of day." Another pause. Sarah hissed at Rollie. "Perhaps," Rollie said, nodding to Sarah, "we might set up publication under our ten-payment plan. Yes—ha ha ha—it *is* sort of like buying furniture, but you're getting the *fame* you deserve this way, Mr. Crispus." Pause. Rollie looked at Sarah. "You think you can swing the cash, eh? Yes, yes, I agree. It's always better to get your obligations out of the way."

Rollie smiled at Sarah. She smiled back. "All right," Rollie said into the phone. "Take a couple of days more to think about it. Next Monday, though, we are preparing our Christmas ads for the *New York Times* and the *New York Herald Tribune*. We have to know by then whether you'll come with us or not—we'd like to give you a lot of space in both papers." Pause. "What? Oh, well, look at it this way, Mr. Crispus. No one could predict the sales of *The Caine Mutiny*, now could they? And look what happened. Incidentally, Mr. Crispus, I was working for the publisher of that book when it came out. I predicted that it would be a best seller— no one else in the office did. No, Mr. Crispus. I have fairly good judgment, but I wouldn't wish to commit myself. You understand? What? Do I think your book has a chance? Mr. Crispus," Rollie said, sounding very sincere, "I would not be calling if I didn't think so. Yes, I do think it'll be a big success. Yes. All right. By Monday. Good-bye. No, no, allow *me* to thank *you*."

Rollie hung up and he poised over the phone for a few seconds. He looked at Sarah. His eyes danced. "I think we'll get it," he said.

"Eight thousand dollars," Sarah said, patting "Rollie's shoulder and looking at him with admiration. "That's like selling a Cadillac. Better."

For the next couple of days Rollie's first words when he walked into the office were, "Did we get the signed contract from Crispus?"

And, of course, one morning we did get it. As soon as we did, Rollie turned without a moment's hesitation to other prospective authors.

Time dragged on. Crispus' book, *O, Come Ye Back*, went to Harriet for editing of a fashion. I heard from Obie. His magazine was really on the skids. His pay days had been delayed a couple of times. A girl I had met joined us one night on the town. Gloria, Obie's girl, was with us too. We should have had a good time, but we didn't. I could see that Obie was spending most of his time thinking about where he would go when the book finally closed.

I thought maybe I could work him into a spot in the office, but I didn't tell him. The chances were I wouldn't be able to make out, what with the cutback in help. Still, there wouldn't be any harm in asking. I would wait for the right time, then ask Rollie.

As it was, being a one-man department, I came, for the very first time, in contact with everything. With the letters from old authors whose books hadn't sold more than five or ten copies; with the newspapers that asked that we stop sending publicity material to them because they wouldn't give space to a book or author published by a vanity house.

Our files, containing tons of letters, gave testimony that Rocket was printing books, little more. The pattern seemed to be that the initial contact with the prospective authors was the sales pitch, and very sincere though it was, it didn't really promise anything. Once a contract was signed, no one bothered about the author. Perhaps the author's letters were answered, perhaps not. The authors—all of them, to a man or woman—wanted to know how well their books were going. They were not content with the autograph parties, radio and television interviews on a local scale. They wanted national acclaim.

Hadn't the report said the reading market was the entire nation and abroad? Hadn't reports named the sources where a book *could* be nationally advertised? And hadn't they in every way implied fame and fortune?

They had.

We mailed to prospective authors an attractive booklet about how to get a book published. In it were pictures of our old authors signing books at autograph parties, being interviewed on radio or television. There were also quotes from people we had published, praising the company before they received their first financial statements, and paste-ups of reviews were included from papers either kind enough or dumb enough to handle and read our books. Copies of past *Times* and *Tribune* ads were also shown with the dates whited out, because the ads were anywhere from three to five years old. Toward the back of the booklet were montages of royalty checks, all of them quite large, because the figures nine times out of ten had been doctored.

The booklet listed many departments: art, production, etc. Actually, we had only editing and production and promotion. Most of the production was done in the printing plant. Promotion and publicity, of course, were always geared to the local market, the author's home town, and it sometimes happened that more than one person from the same town published through Rocket. Then promotion became a farce.

Once I became aware of the total organization and its methods, I began to ride Rollie just a little. I wanted that raise, but I also wanted to set him up to ask about Obie. Rollie kept evading me.

Then one afternoon, returning from lunch, it came to me. No wonder I had so little trouble getting the job with Rocket. I was up for grabs. It wasn't my skill and experience that counted at all. It was my economic position. I was cheap labor and had no bargaining position. From then on I was angry most of the time.

I had two reasons for being angry. The first was that Rollie and Sarah had taken advantage of the times. They could pay me less because I wouldn't be able to get a similar job with a reputable firm without a great deal of luck. They weren't really afraid I'd leave—they knew that for Negroes, white-collar jobs, especially in my profession, didn't come easily.

The second was the businesslike way Rollie went about fleecing people—old, young or in-between, it didn't matter to him. Once a contract was signed, the legal department could follow through if the author decided to pull out. That part of the contract was airtight in Rocket's favor. It made me angry that Rollie could be ruthless with people's dreams. Being a dreamer, I knew how important, sometimes even more than life itself, dreams can be.

Almost every day after this revelation, I was in conflict with

Rollie. I wanted him to do just a little bit more for the authors, like using good stock for publicity blurbs instead of the cheap, tiny cards we used. I wanted signs printed for use in the author's home town instead of the ragged, unattractive posters made of strips of colored paper we sent out.

But Rollie always said no.

Once a week he asked if I would see a show with him.

I always said no.

So there was still another reason for being angry. I could have got my raise, sure. All I had to do was be nice to Rollie. Mostly, however, I was angry and sorry for the little people who had taken all their savings in order to publish a volume of their lousy poetry or memoirs. People like Rollie and Sarah look down their noses at cannibals who, at least, have something in their cultures which made them that way. It was a little frightening to think that there was something infinitely worse festering in our culture to have allowed specimens like Rollie and Sarah not only to survive but to thrive on their brand of cannibalism.

And one day after a sleepless night, I complained to Rollie about his wanting me to fabricate reports to old authors—to list things we had done for them, but in reality had not—and to frame the reports in such a manner that they could not be checked.

Rollie, I think, had had almost enough of me. He wasn't smiling when he said, "What's the matter with you? Just pad the reports like I asked you. Be careful what you say. It's a job; what the hell."

Sarah, standing there, nodding in agreement, said, "It's a job, so you'll not worry about it."

I could feel myself getting sick from holding in the anger, not showing it in a healthy way. But when you know that the next day you may be out of work, stuck at home puttering around while people all over the city are rushing to and from jobs, your answers come slowly, if at all. Your anger, sealed by expediency, returns to the depths inside and begins to burn away. Then the fear comes and you suspect every lowered voice, every glance in your direction, and you become almost functionless thinking, they will fire me before I can find something else.

I knew I'd better spend some time looking around for a new job. I was thinking that as I left Rollie and Sarah and returned slowly to my own desk. Leah gave me some of her coffee. Harriet looked inquiringly toward me, but said nothing. I stared out over Bryant Park, not really seeing anything.

Suddenly panic slammed into me. What if Rollie and Sarah, *right at that moment*, were deciding to fire me? What if they said, "Get the hell out?"

I think I was nearly trembling when I sat down and buzzed Leah. "Look, doll," I said. "Let me talk to Rollie."

He was pleased, yes, he was pleased that I had time that week to see a show with him. In fact, he was delighted. He said so.

CHAPTER NINE

I SAT UP smoking all that night, smoking and thinking. In the morning I had it. All right, I'd make that "date" with Rollie in order to secure my job for a little while. In addition to that, I'd find out if he would take Obie in.

Obie and I had lunch and I talked with him about Rocket. I didn't tell him about Rollie. I didn't think he'd understand how great my fear was of being on the streets again. Maybe he did, I don't know, but I didn't say anything.

I told Obie there might be an outside chance of my swinging him into the company. He listened without expression.

"If I can do it, it'll only be part-time," I said.

He still said nothing. He sort of smiled at his plate. Then he looked up. "Man," he said, "you know something?"

"What?"

"Thanks for looking out for me but, Steve, I'm just not interested in shoveling shit for a crooked-paddy company. After all you've told me about that place, well . . . *later*."

"It's just something for eating money, man. You know that."

"I'm wise. Steve, in a few days or weeks I'm going to be out here on my ass again. I know what I'm capable of doing and the people who interview me know it too. I'm through making compromises because I'm Negro. I've made hundreds of them, just like you, and I know that after a while making the compromise becomes a habit and you're always knee-deep in it, always, always."

I thought of the "date" with Rollie. "Yeah," I said.

Obie chuckled derisively. "It's a damned shame. A Negro can always get into something no good or not going anywhere. He tells himself it's temporary, but you check out all the post offices in America—New York, Chicago, Atlanta, Los Angeles—graveyards of Negro talent, every goddam one of 'em, where some cat has gone in for a little while to get the weight off his ass, and there he stays, having made his compromise, which, my man, is considerably better than Rocket."

"You kiss my ass," I told Obie. He was burning me up with his talk. Indirectly, it all reflected on me.

Obie became serious. "You're near it too, man. No more compromises."

"I like to eat," I grumbled.

"Who doesn't? But after a while it won't matter except when you get light-headed and have headaches. Later, even these you don't mind."

"Goddam it, Obie. You don't have to tell me!"

"What's eatin' you, man? What you been smokin'?"

"Shut the hell up," I said. "I'll give you some of my part-time contacts when your book gets to the knitty-gritty. I guess that'll be clean enough for you."

"So that's it."

I tamped a cigarette hard against the table and said nothing.

"Aw, man, I didn't mean anything personal. Let's get the hell out of here."

I was still thinking of the conversation with Obie when I met Rollie a couple of nights later for dinner and a show. With the coming of night he seemed even more effeminate; he practically sparkled. He brought up the raise, not me. He said with a little laugh, "You'll probably take this chance to push for your raise. We might be able to get it, but we can talk about it later."

As we plowed our way through steaks, I noticed that he kept looking up and I had the feeling that he wanted to see someone looking at us. I forgot it because he began talking about the race thing.

"I think it's terrible," he said, "that a man can't get a decent break in this country because he happens to be black. At Rocket, as you know, Steve, we hire people for their skills. Color doesn't mean a damned thing to us."

I listened to his crap and my stomach became so knotted up that I had to quit halfway through the steak. But he went on. "My mother raised me—my father died—and she taught me that the worth of a man could not be measured in color. Wonderful woman."

We had a couple of martinis apiece before dinner. They went to work on Rollie during dessert. He smiled across the table at me and said. "You're something of an athlete, aren't you—or weren't you?"

The question surprised me. I looked at him without saying anything.

"You walk like it," he said. "Gracefully, manfully. You move beautifully, Steve."

And I said to myself, Oh, crap. Walking to the theatre after dinner, I was on edge. I tensed each time he walked close enough to me to brush arms. Rollie, on the other hand, was chatting, gesturing, doing everything as brilliantly as the sexiest doll you ever laid eyes on. I thought when we got in the theatre it would be a little better. It wasn't.

Rollie must have stroked my arm at least fifty times as he made his comments on the play. Once he pushed his fingers into my bicep. They lingered there until I moved my arm. I felt that everyone in the place was watching, not the play, but us, and I damned near ran out of there at the first intermission.

We smoked in the lobby, Rollie standing very close to me, as though he would charm me. Once he gripped my wrist, like a woman, as he turned to point something out to me, and once, in a cold anger, I took his upper arm. He smiled, pleased, and I smiled too as I squeezed until he jumped. I wanted him to feel the strength and hate there. I wanted the pressure to say to him what I was afraid to speak with my mouth.

"You're strong," he said.

"Let's go sit down," I said disgustedly.

Some of the message must have gotten to him because he kept his hands in his lap during the next act. At intermission he seemed nervous. He kept looking at me as though he wanted to say something. He knew I knew what that something was. The "later" he had talked of when he spoke about the raise had not come—yet. I knew it had to come and it did at the end of the show.

As we left the theatre, Rollie suggested drinks at his place as though it were mere formality—that it had already been settled. He was relieved when I didn't argue. We hopped a cab and took off.

"How'd you like it?" he asked me.

"All right," I answered. The cab wheeled through the streets toward the East Side.

"I thought it was great," he said.

"We'll be talking about the raise," I said. "Won't we?"

"Yes, yes, of course," he said.

The cab driver was Negro. A couple of times I looked into the mirror and our eyes met. I wondered what he was thinking. I wanted to say something that would tell him that it wasn't what it looked like, but Rollie, perhaps sensing what was on my mind, said in a low voice, "You look very handsome tonight, Steve. I like that suit."

I could have killed him. Instead I said, "You look pretty cute yourself."

He gave me a reproachful look, but I turned and stared into the streets until the cab stopped in the East 60's. He guided me up the steps and into his building. I couldn't help thinking of the little old ladies and the arthritic old men and young frustrated writers who'd made living in this neighborhood possible for Rollie.

I nearly choked when I saw his place. I had no idea he lived so well. Peter du Jardin-type furniture was all around. The rugs were in decorator colors and you felt as if you'd sink to your knees if you moved. Everything in the place was beautiful, but somehow a sense of loneliness pervaded the apartment. It seemed to me that anything as lovely as Rollie's apartment should have been shared with a woman. I thought, for a part of a second, of Grace and me moving about the place—that it was ours, and Frank and Teddy were sunk in the rugs watching the television set.

Rollie finished showing me around and I sat down while he went to fix drinks. Of course, I thought with a smile, this is just the sort of layout some young boo-hoo packer would like to have. And there would be Rollie, of course, to give him spending change. All the packer had to do would be to be around when it was packing time. But maybe Rollie's particular narcissism didn't include having anyone hanging around until the time.

He had changed into tight black pants and a white silk shirt cut like the ones Bob Cummings wears on his television show. He explained this when he brought the drinks by saying, "I wanted to get into something more comfortable."

He sat down beside me and looked at me lingeringly.

"Well, how about it?" I asked.

"How about what?"

"The raise, Rollie. Isn't that why we're here?"

He took a sip of his drink. He wasn't pleased, but I was damned tired of him thinking he was rowing *this* boat.

"Drink," he said. "Don't drive so hard. We'll get to it."

"I hope so," I said. I was tired. I hadn't realized how much of a strain it had been being with him most of the evening. I was tired and getting, as they used to say at home, "evil."

Obie wasn't on my mind anymore—I didn't have to worry about being nice to get him a job. That left just me, and, sipping the drink,

I knew damned well that I could scuffle just as well as Obie, so my fear ran on off.

"How about another drink?" I asked Rollie.

He seemed very glad to hear that and he bounded up and wiggled into the kitchen. I watched him, thinking he didn't wiggle that way in the office. He had refilled his glass, too, and he was very gay when he sat down again. I decided to have some fun with him.

"You look very cute in that outfit," I said.

He ran his hands along the tight black pants. "You like it?" he asked. He was pleased to hell and back.

"It's a knockout," I said, sipping my drink.

"I can get you a shirt like this," he volunteered.

"Not my style, baby," I answered.

"What?"

"I said it wasn't my style, baby."

"Say it again."

"What?"

"Baby."

"Why?"

"I like the way you say it."

I took another sip of the drink and very carefully placed the glass on the table in front of us. I half-turned toward him and said, "Baby."

He moved toward me, his drink splashing all over the couch. I moved away, pushing him gently against the shoulder.

"The raise," I said. "The raise."

"You bastards always want something, don't you?" he said huskily.

"I have it coming and you know it."

"What do you want?"

"Minimum. A bill a week."

"Oh, come now, Steve. You know we can't pay you that."

"That's what I want. Now what do you want?"

"Can you imagine? He had the nerve enough to try to blush.

"We can't pay you that," he repeated softly. He touched my arm; his hand tightened on it. He tried to move toward me.

73

"But that's what I want, baby," I said, "I got to have it."

"Take a little less," he said with a pleading look in his eyes.

"Can't. Got to have a bill a week."

"Let me work it out with Sarah and the people downtown."

"Uh-uh. Now, baby. Now."

Exasperated, he jumped up. "I tell you, Steve, I can't."

I stood up. "Better be going," I said.

Rollie sped around in front of me as I started for the door. "Don't go. Don't go. Why do you need so much money? Money isn't everything."

"Can I go now?" I asked. "Can I go, baby?"

I had counted on the bastard melting, but he didn't. Instead he slipped inside my arms, quickly, deftly, like a woman, and his face came closer to mine. I could smell the Yardley's. I was fascinated as I would be fascinated by the sight of a huge snake.

"Back up, baby," I said. "Back up."

Now he closed his eyes and thrust himself forward. I backed up and came off my right foot, driving my right fist beside his mouth. Rollie was jolted to one side. He hit the wall and slid down to the floor. He wasn't out. As I passed him, he kind of smiled with his eyes and, downstairs, in the street, I wondered if he liked that sort of thing. Hard to tell about people.

Well, Obie, I thought, you got yourself some company, I suppose. I didn't figure Rollie would fire me the next day, but fire me he would, and I had to find something before he did.

The fear came again and it didn't diminish when I told myself that I would find something.

CHAPTER TEN

I HAD LITTLE time to eat on my lunch hours. I went all over town on job interviews, and met all kinds of people. I tried not disclosing my race, which was in accordance with the law, but when that didn't seem to work out, I attempted to save myself time and trouble by advising the interviewer beforehand that I was Negro. When I didn't tell them, they were very often surprised when they saw me. They explained that I hadn't sounded like a Negro on the phone.

What I disliked most was to be mistaken for a messenger. In New York, great numbers of messengers are Negro. You see them everywhere in mid and downtown. Usually they are well-dressed, neat-appearing young men, and so was I. At least twenty times I was asked to leave the package. The package was my folio. I couldn't help but smile sometimes, thinking how universal the conditioning of the white man is. All Negroes look alike or, in this instance, all neat-appearing young men look alike because they're Negro and they must all be, of course, messengers.

I met some good people who I am sure considered me on my merits and found me not right for the job. There were always, however, too few of these people.

Sometimes tests were given during the interviews. I disliked taking them. In my case a test was a waste of time because the interviewer knew all the time that the job wouldn't be mine in any event. But to keep up appearances and comply with the law, he had to give the test. You return it in a day or so and they tell you they'll call. The chances are pretty good that you'll never see or hear about the sample copy you did. "Samples" of this sort can create such a backlog for the employer that he wouldn't have to hire writers at all.

I wasn't having any luck at all. Sometimes, realizing I was pressing, I eased up and didn't bother with interviews for a while. I would suddenly get the image of myself sitting in an office with a chip on my shoulder. If not that, just sitting there as though I didn't really care about getting the job. I was sure some of this must have been communicated to the people who interviewed me, so I forgot about the rounds for a while, just kept my ears open and stuck it out at Rocket where things between Rollie and me had become very chilly. Nothing much was happening except Leah's birthday and the production of Crispus' book.

The presses were pretty well filled and it was going to be difficult to squeeze O, Come Ye Back on. It was just waiting. The expectation of Leah's birthday party we were going to hold in the office carried me through three or four bad days. The day before the party I found a tremendous coffee mug upon which I had painted Leah's name. For her it was an ideal present. Rollie and Sarah stayed a little later than usual the day of the party, but then they finally realized they were putting a damper on it and they left.

Some of Leah's friends stopped in and I was expecting my date, a friend of Gloria's. We had a nice little crowd going. The Old Grandad had never been better, although I could have used Scotch for a change. My co-workers were hardier types, it seemed; even Anne was really drinking. Across the way the Empire State Building sparkled like a new scepter set with precious stones. It was quite beautiful, I thought, my head just a little light. I had a warm, satisfying feeling across my chest. Nice.

The party was half over when I began to feel uneasy. It was the way Harriet kept looking at me. Once Leah sidled over and said, "You'd better watch that Harriet. She's got eyes for you." Her tone was light and she might have been jesting, but I didn't think so. I looked closely at her. She smiled, but her eyes stayed the same. I recalled her phrase, "Kidding on the square."

Harriet was telling jokes now, all of them a little lewd, and I know some lewdies. From time to time she looked at me and I wished my date would hurry. We all laughed politely at Harriet's jokes. She began to dominate the party more and more. She was drinking like a fish. When the girls walked past her to get a drink or something, Harriet whacked them across the rump and cried, "Whaddaya say, keed?" The girls said, "Harriet, stop."

She got up and stood next to me. "Steve, you and me are the only ones puttin' this stuff away, eh?"

"Yeah, we do pretty good," I said.

Then she leaned on me, her withered arm thrusting into my side. I didn't want to move for fear of embarrassing her. When she talked to me, she tilted her face upwards and her eyes roamed restlessly over mine. I wished again that my date would hurry, be just a little early for the late dinner we were going to have. I felt if I called her while the party was going on full blast, it might get Harriet off me, so I did. There was no answer and I guessed she was on her way. The party began to break up. People drifted out until only Harriet and I remained.

"I'd better go downstairs," I said, "and meet my girl." I began to slip on my jacket.

"Aw, wait for her up here, Stevie boy."

Stevie boy, I thought. "No, I'd better go down."

"Let's see how the city looks with our lights out," she said, flicking off the switch. She stumbled in my direction, taking the long way to the window, passing very close to where I stood. I prayed for Evalyn to burst in.

"Come and look," Harriet said, taking my hand.

I let my hand lie in hers for a minute. When I thought she was relaxed, I tried to slip it away. She stood facing the window as if enraptured by the view, then she turned to me. I couldn't step backwards—my desk was directly behind me. She shoved herself at me so hard, I grunted. With her one good arm she put a headlock on me, brought my head down and tried to kiss me. I was ducking and weaving all over hell.

"Quit, Harriet!"

She was strong. She nubbed me in the back with her game arm. If I had pushed her, she'd have gone through the window. I twisted around so that she was away from it. I tried to pry her off. The feel and the smell of her disgusted me.

"Steve boy—just a kiss, Stevie . . ."

I remembered her scraggly gray hair, her long yellowed teeth. She was comparatively harmless before the bourbon; at least she was able to behave. Now she was like a comic-strip character coming to life in a dirty book. We struggled. I tried not to hurt her, tried to watch out for the window, and all the time she kept hissing at me, trying to bite me. Finally I forced her away and she said, "You nigger, you." We both panted. She brushed her hair back and said in a desperate bitter voice, "Oh, Stevie, c'mon. Don't you want to? To a *white* woman? I won't tell. I won't tell." She began unbuttoning her blouse. She changed her mind and began pulling drunkenly at the hem of her skirt.

I thrust her back against the wall and held her there, breathing hard. I could see her whole life then, of loving so many guys, of wanting so many guys, of not wanting to be alone with her aunt always, yet saying nothing because of the arm.

"Harriet," I said. "Listen to me. No, now, please stop. You're just a little high."

She relaxed, and for just a fraction of a second I wanted to hit her, smash her against that wall. I ran out feeling weak and sick and very glad I hadn't hit her in anger. I shuddered thinking about being arrested on a rape charge. Would the cops believe that a middle-aged woman with an arm crippled by polio had tried to rape *me*? Yeah, they would!

I met my date Evalyn as I rushed blindly out of the building. Dinner went badly. My mind wasn't on it. I kept thinking of my vulnerability and I wondered what life would be like with a white face. I took Evalyn home and returned to my place and again I wasn't able to sleep too much.

The next day and for a few days afterward, it was pretty miserable being in the office around Harriet and Rollie. I didn't mention the incident to Harriet and she didn't talk about it either, not even to apologize. Leah, I think, sensed something, but she had the good grace not to ask what. Anne, on the other hand, always rather crude, said several times, "Well, what's the matter with you two?"

Sometimes I caught Harriet wiping her eyes hastily. It wouldn't have done any good for me to have said. "Aw, hell, forget it," so I didn't. A part of me went out to her, and I could feel for her endlessly drab life. But another part of me smoldered. I mean, hers and Rollie's behavior was just another case of using me. In every conceivable manner they want to use you. I felt this more than sympathy for Harriet.

What with the job and all, I was really mixed up and I would have cracked up had it not been for Lois.

But let me explain. The first girl friend I had was Sally Ricci. She lived upstairs over us with her family. When she and the other girls in the neighborhood played house, I was drafted to play father. It seemed the games of soldiers and cowboys and Indians bored me, although Sally's brother, Nick, usually came to urge me away from the girls. But you don't get any kicks playing soldier. Sally always played the mother, and I the father. We would send the kids who played with us to the movies or to school, as our parents did, and then we would be parents ourselves down there in the cool cellar. Sally and I got along well together.

Sally had auburn hair and gray eyes, and when I first saw Lois on the bus, I thought, This is how Sally must look now. Another thing about Lois. From a distance she reminded me of Lint's wife, Bobbie. I saw Lois about three mornings a week. You couldn't help but see her. She was the type of woman everyone stares at when she gets on a bus or into a subway car. Her hair was cut short and her brows were arched just slightly, like twin beautiful streams of mist. Her complexion was flawless. Her lips were red and full; they looked very warm and soft. Then you saw the gray eyes and they had about them a tender, warming look that made you want to walk fences.

If there were no seats, she stood in the aisle, her trim legs spread slightly while she looked through a window. You could see she was a little embarrassed when people looked at her. She was beautiful, the most beautiful woman I've ever seen. And two or three mornings a week she got off at my stop, Fifth and 42nd, and vanished in the swirling crowds.

Sometimes I saw her on the evening bus. We never spoke, of course, except to say, "Excuse me," going for a seat or moving back. I seldom got a seat. The harmless-looking old ladies trampled me to death. It was safer to stand still and cover up. If I did get a seat, I would look up over my paper to where Lois was standing and find her looking at me, which was, perhaps, what had made me look up. As Obie would have said, "Something flowing in the air" between us. I wanted badly to say something to her, but who in New York or anywhere else opens by saying, "I noticed you on the bus"?

Then I was out early on a Saturday morning, one of those warm fall days when the sun sparkles like old gold and you hate to stay indoors. I had been out walking around the park with Lint, listening to his complaints about Bobbie—when I was with her, she complained about him—and I thought the day much too fine to listen long to either of them.

I hurried home.

On the way I saw Lois coming out of a little store with two bags of groceries. Each bag seemed almost as big as she. Her back was arched with the weight of them, and as I walked behind her I could see her straining in her tight, black knee-length pants and striped T-shirt. Again I was struck by her resemblance to Bobbie. Lois heard my footsteps and turned. Her face brightened instantly. I tried to keep mine expressionless. I swung out to go past. My stride broke.

"Can I help you with one of those?" I heard myself say. I looked at her. God, she was beautiful.

"Would you mind awfully?"

I took the largest of the two bags. It was heavy. I looked at her. She didn't seem that strong, but I guessed she was.

"Heavy, isn't it?"

"I'll say," I smiled. We walked in silence a half a block. When we got in front of my apartment building I automatically paused.

"You live here, don't you?" she said.

"Yes," I said. She had stopped too.

She wrinkled her face. "I live at the end of the block. It isn't too far. Can you—would you mind—"

"—awfully," I finished for her.

We laughed and shifted the bags, then walked on, looking at

80

one another out of the corners of our eyes and smiling. When we got to her building we passed a Negro doorman who said, "That's a pretty big delivery boy you got there, Miss Fleck."

"He's not a delivery boy, Dan. He's a friend." She smiled brightly at me.

The doorman and I sized each other up in a glance, then Lois and I went into the elevator. She placed her bag on the floor.

"Why don't you put your bag down? We have to go all the way to the top. It's cheaper up there."

"Why didn't you have this stuff delivered?" I asked.

"I'd have had to wait too long for them. I needed some things right away."

We got to the top. "I can't thank you enough," she said when we were inside her place. It was four times larger than mine.

"What's this cost you?" I couldn't help asking it.

She told me. It was the same amount I paid for my place. It didn't make me angry; it made me sad, and I shook my head.

"I've seen you on the bus a lot," she said, and right away I thought, Oh, she said it. "I'm glad you weren't on it today. I don't know how I'd have made it home."

"I'm glad I wasn't on it," I said.

She smiled and clasped her hands together in front of her. I couldn't help smiling back.

"Would you like some coffee?" she said.

"I'd love it," I said.

"All right. You go in there and sit down. Be ready in a minute." She began to flutter all over the place. Her apartment overlooked Riverside Drive. I could see the park, the river, and across it, the Palisades.

"What's your name?" she shouted from the kitchen.

"Steve! What's yours?"

"Lois!" She came out seconds later with a glass of cold beer. "Lois Fleck."

"Hill," I said, taking the beer with some surprise.

"Coffee's not ready yet," she explained. "You do drink beer, don't you?"

"Sure."

"What kind of work do you do?" she asked. She sat down. "You get off at Fifth and Forty-second—I think."

I told her what I did. I didn't tell her what sort of company Rocket was though. When I finished I said, "You seem to notice a lot of things."

She smiled and got up to see about the coffee. She came back walking slowly, as if to give an idea time to nurture. "You have anything to do this afternoon?"

"No," I said, though Obie and I had tentatively thought about a football game.

"Like to stay for dinner?" Then she said hastily, "I assume you're not married and you either eat out or cook yourself."

"I'm not married and I'd love to stay for dinner someone else cooks."

"Good," she said with a smile. "You won't mind if I make something fabulous, would you?"

"No. Can I help?"

"Can you peel potatoes?"

"Sure."

We went into the kitchen. Just like that, we had been caught up in each other. In the kitchen she gave me an apron and put me to work. She seemed very happy to have someone to talk with. She was very animated. It was delightful for me. There was no strain, no pain. Lois understood what I talked about almost before I said it, and several times we hit upon the crux of an idea at the same time and stood grinning at each other, quite proud of ourselves.

I learned a lot about Lois and her family that afternoon. The Flecks had come from Austria, fleeing before Hitler moved in to take the country. They had come to New York and her father had gone into business. One of his shops was in Harlem. I was silent for a second or two thinking about that shop in Harlem. Lois chattered on. She had gone to C.C.N.Y. and came out of Liberal Arts. She was a Gal Friday in one of those hustling little ad agencies. She worked in ceramics on the side. Her parents were orthodox

Jews. I had known many when I was a kid. I used to make pin money during the holidays by lighting the gas for them. Since Lois went to school, worked with and knew many Christians, her folks watched her carefully. They didn't want her to marry one and they protested vigorously when she dated them while she lived at home.

Lois' parents were Old World Jews; Lois was not. She'd spent her formative years in America and almost from the start had relinquished much of the tradition of her parents. She, too, had to belong. But the pressures from both directions created problems that drove her into analysis. She could not quite decide whether she should live her own life or live it for her parents. She finally decided she had to live it for herself and she moved away from home. Sometimes she wasn't sure she was right. Her mother sounded like a witch.

"What's *your* mother like?" she asked. She was a little wistful, and I guessed she thought it had not been wise to begin the conversation.

"A little like yours."

"Oh, no."

"Perhaps not."

"I'll bet she's wise and kind. She's a good cook and you love her very much."

"I guess so."

We sat down to eat and she put on a stack of records. It was all very nice. Lois and I talked with our eyes. When we spoke aloud, the words were few. As I stood at the door, looking deep into those gray eyes, I knew I would see her again and I felt quite sure she wanted to see me. It was all over to quickly, but I didn't have any idea how soon I was to see her again.

I passed the doorman on the way out and he smiled. I glared back at him, but I think I was a little pleased that he thought what I knew he was thinking. We said nothing, yet it was as if there was complete understanding between us, like there is on the buses when Negroes get on and don't sit beside each other. They spread out, making those whites who don't wish to sit beside Negroes uncomfortable. The understanding, though unspoken, is the same.

I rushed home to call Obie. He cussed me out. I suggested we make it to The Bird—Birdland—since I had goofed on the game. We arranged to meet just outside.

CHAPTER ELEVEN

WE DASHED inside Birdland, Obie and I, and halfway down the steps he said, "Who's on the bill?"

"I don't know," I said. "I thought you knew."

We trotted back upstairs and checked the boards.

"Never heard of them," Obie said, "but Powell's on too, so we'll catch him."

We went back downstairs and got seats in the gallery next to the rail. Bud Powell came on. He blinked and took his seat at the piano. Obie and I sat there listening. At one point, Obie leaned over the rail and whispered, "Blow, Bud, blow."

Powell winked and nodded. His fingers ran over the keys, and as he worked out his innovations he bent closer and closer to the piano. Satisfied, he raised his head and looked up at the ceiling. For me, Powell could play all night. We decided to stay through and catch him again.

Obie and I were returning from the bar to reclaim our seats from the tourist trade when a small group of musicians sauntered onstage. They spoke softly to one another and moved restlessly. Then, almost by accident, it seemed, they began to play. Their shadows loomed huge behind them. They seemed like mannikins on the stage, oblivious to the complex sounds they were making, unaware of the emotions they stirred.

Obie began to tap on the table with a forefinger, I looked around. People were nodding to the beat. I turned back to the stage and watched the brown fingers of the bass player. They moved in a tireless, throbbing rhythm. The eyes of the youth—he was no more than twenty-two–stared into the crowd in front of him as though he were searching for someone or something he'd lost. All of a sudden I couldn't help shaking my head gently from side to side. I heard someone keeping a ragged footbeat. I was surprised to find it was me.

The trumpet player moved forward on the stage then. At first I wasn't sure what he was playing. The notes were soft and fluid, rolling swiftly with hardly a noticeable break. The tune seemed almost obscured. Finally I realized it was "Skylark." It had been popular around 1942. In utter concentration the trumpeter peered through half-closed eyes at his fingers on the valves; they might have been acting independent of him. Behind the trumpet, the piano chorded softly and the bass became the flap of bird's wings on a summer mid-morning.

The picture of what they were doing was clear in my mind now. The alto sax man pivoted slightly and began to blow with a gentle rush of air. The trumpeter, receiving applause from the crowd, gave a single, almost sardonic nod and stepped to the side, where he sleepily filled in the breaks of the saxophone with soft, echoing notes. Here the skylark swam effortlessly across the sky, diving among the trees, coming to rest for a second on the lower branches, stopping to pick up something in its beak.

Some of the words were running through my mind when the sax man quit abruptly, and the piano player, hunched over the keys in a posture of restrained eagerness, placed the skylark drifting and dipping on the currents of air. The trumpeter and the saxophonist, standing on different sides of the stand and peering coolly down at the audience, pointed and counterpointed each other on the theme, their triplets, flatted fifths and diminished ninths filling in with eerie shadows the portrait of the bird and the lovers waiting for it.

Applause filled the room.

Obie said, "What do you think?"

"Pretty good," I said.

"Damned good," he said.

We turned quickly back to the stage. A bongo player slipped into the lights and, crouched over his drums, began beating a soft, rapid rhythm which stilled the uneven sounds of talking in the crowd. The audience became ready to absorb the music, to go into it. The trumpeter and the saxophonist set the theme and broke off suddenly, leaving a void into which the bongo player rushed, his hands making pale blurs above the small drums clutched tightly between his knees.

"Go, bongo!" someone shouted.

There seemed a hundred insinuating beats coming all at once from beneath the hands of the drummer. Faster. The spotlight came up full. I could see Obie's head shaking to the beat. I began tapping the table myself, but it seemed not enough. Faster. The dry irritating thuds slammed into the room. The head of the bongo player bent forward so that his black hair dangled loose and shook in black strings as he tore his head left and right, pausing only at the end of a few bars to throw back his head and suck air through his clenched teeth. The bass fell in then, with an ominous, heavy beat which seemed a thing racing through complete blackness. The sound of a hundred feet tapping softly became pronounced. I recalled how the floor of the high-school gym had swung, swayed and creaked to the measured, deathless beat of dancing while our team dressed beneath it after a basketball game.

The bongo player hit four rapid beats so close together they were as one. Simultaneously, the bass player quit and there lingered in the air a horrible, empty sound. Then, almost with a sneer, the sax man moved into the center of the stage. He blew insinuating, insulting notes. He broke off, curved them, picked up the threads and wove them back into a theme.

At one point I had the image of a great horse galloping across a land shrouded in darkness, his name streaming behind him. Right behind that image I had another one of something soft and gentle, a beautiful thing. Again through counterpoint, the trumpeter and the saxophonist wove the weird, haunting sound into the melody.

I suddenly felt warm beneath my armpits; I could feel moisture on my body. The notes from the horns matched, grew loud, leaped on a flat fifth and quit. The bongo player, almost forgotten, hit four soft beats and flung his head over his drums. A second or two elapsed before the crowd knew the number was over; then it burst into wild applause.

"Man," Obie said. "Let's get out of here. That action left me limp."

"We went next door to William's for some ribs. We ate in silence until Obie said, "You're kind of quiet. What's happening?"

"Nothing," I said. I had been listening to the music. It was the same stuff Lois had played.

"You turn up anything yet?" he asked.

"Not a goddam thing."

After a pause Obie said, "This is a funny town. You never really know what's going on."

"Yeah."

"Cleveland's supposed to be a crazy place."

"So I heard, but this is the place, man, New York."

Obie was silent for a minute. Then he said, "You know what we should do?"

"What?"

"Start an ad or PR agency—make it go so we don't have to be dependent on other people for a living."

"An agency—" I began.

"Yes," he said. "I know what you're thinking. What're we going to eat—where's the money coming from to set it up—where are we going to get accounts from? I know that's what you're thinking."

"Yeah."

"It's the only way out of this crap," he said.

"That's no way out," I said, thinking of the little, darkroomed Negro agencies I'd seen from New York to Los Angeles.

Obie said, "I guess we're too afraid of starving, and yet, look what's happened to us already. Man, if we don't get a couple of things soon we'll be starving anyway. And there's nothing sure about what we will be doing."

"I guess not, Obie, but there ought to be something."

"I go for the idea of not having a boss who can walk in and fire me at any time."

"Jesus, Obie, who doesn't?"

Obie rushed on. "We could work exclusively in the Negro market. We'd be experts."

"Man," I said heatedly, "I thought we talked about this before? Negro market—that's sixteen million niggers each with ten dollars in his pocket. Big deal. You got ten dollars, Obie?"

"Aw, man—"

"And even if there was a market, Obie, why would you want to prolong the goddam isolation. Look at you, look what isolation did for you. Top man in the class and look at you! Obie, damn it, look at us!"

"I'm looking," he said.

"In another ten or fifteen years it would be gone anyway. It'll be absorbed into the total market. It's inevitable."

Obie threw down his fork. "Aw, hell, let's walk, man."

We dragged around Broadway, getting our kicks watching the tourists. We listened to the rush of water pouring down the Pepsi-Cola sign; we watched the huge, mechanized Johnny Walker striding smilingly west with his swinging cane, and we saw the Anheuser-Busch horses trampling red and soundless out of the night. Around us people sludged along, gaping, staring all around. We stopped in a bar on Seventh Avenue and began to drink Scotch shorties with beer, but I couldn't get to feeling good. We decided to call it a night.

I went home to my apartment and shut out the Saturday night. I fixed coffee and smoked. I showered and thumbed through the paper, but I couldn't concentrate on it. I put it aside and reached for the phone book. I thumbed through it looking for the F's, then the Fl's. The phone rang. The bell was turned low and the ringing sounded very intimate, very special.

"Hello," I said.

"Want to go for a walk? I don't feel like walking alone."

"Huh?"

She laughed.

"Lois?"

"Yes. I tried to call you before. Are you alone?"

"Yes." I reached for a cigarette, lighted it.

"You want to?"

"What? Oh, walk. All right. I'll be right down."

"If you're tired," she said, "forget it. I'm so stupid for calling at this hour."

"No," I said. "I guess I hoped you would. Matter of fact—"

"Yes?"

"Nothing." I stared around the apartment.

"You did?"

"Did what?"

"Hope I would call?"

"Yes."

"Isn't it supposed to be the other way around?"

"Well—"

"Do you know how many times I called you?"

"No."

"Three times, I'm afraid. I thought it quite foolish, but I couldn't stop once I got the notion."

I was silent for a while. Then I said, "I'll be right down."

I dressed and went out. She was standing in her lobby. I could see her through the glass door with her gray flannel slacks and brown buckskin jacket. She wore a black scarf around her neck. She started to move the instant she saw me; she was smiling. I smiled back. We walked across the street and leaned on the stone wall. It was a bit chilly, but otherwise nice. Lois took several deep breaths and turned to me, smiling again. The sky was clear and star-filled. The river moved in shadows. Across it, the big Spry sign flashed red and white. Cars rushed by on the parkway, their lights lancing up bolder and bolder, then vanishing suddenly. We walked down to 79th Street, then into the park. We sat on a bench and lighted cigarettes.

"What did you do tonight?" she asked.

I told her.

"I've never been to Birdland," she said. "I went to Basin Street once, though."

"I'll take you sometime."

"Promise."

"I promise."

"I'd love it."

We stared out over the river. Small blocks of light stood on the edges of the Palisades from the buildings there.

"What do you usually do Saturday nights?" I asked.

She shrugged, "I do nothing usually. I date sometimes. Two or three times a week."

"Nice Jewish home-type boys?"

She cracked up. When she stopped laughing she asked, "And you?"

"Yeah, I date sometimes."

"New York can be terribly lonely on a Saturday night if you've nothing to do, nowhere to go."

"Yes," I said. "I know." I could see she considered me a neuter— nice to be with, wonderful to talk to, excellent company for a lonely girl.

"It's beautiful like this, isn't it?" she said.

"Yes," I said, but I was looking at her. She was very beautiful in the soft, almost morning light. I wanted to take her hand. I don't think she would have minded, but I didn't. We walked back up along the Drive and sat down again. It was about four, but I was not really tired.

"I could use some coffee," I said. "How about you?"

"Could I! Do you have any?"

Right away we both knew she shouldn't have said that, but I jumped up before she could say anything and said, "Just made a fresh pot. C'mon."

She came.

She smiled as she walked slowly through the door of my place. "I thought," she said, "it would look like this. Yes, I've been imagining all sorts of things about you."

I lighted the coffee and put Oscar Peterson's "Autumn in New York" on the player; it's great at four in the morning.

"Dance?" I said.

Lois hesitated for a moment, then came into my arms, her eyes a little wide. She felt very good. She held her arm way out. I took it and drew it in a little.

"Going to fly away?" I asked.

She laughed nervously and was very relieved when the record was through playing. I shut the player off and turned the radio on. We had coffee, then more. It was getting close to five. I kept thinking. Something has to happen.

"I think I'd better go," she said. She walked to the door and stood there. She looked at me inquiringly.

"Good night," I said. "It was nice."

"Wait a minute," she said. "Aren't you going to walk me home?"

"No," I said. Something had told me that this was the right thing to say.

"You're kidding, Steve."

"No, I'm not."

"Good night, then." She went out.

It would have been nice to walk her home, to be with her a few minutes longer just to see what happened.

I had just got into bed when the phone rang.

Lois said, "You're a bastard, you know it?"

"Yes."

"A nice bastard."

I smiled to myself. "Can I call you sometime?"

"Yes."

A silence followed her rather positive assent.

"Fine," I said. "Good night."

"Good night, Steve."

CHAPTER TWELVE

I DIDN'T see Lois on the bus the next morning. I guess I expected to.

Harriet didn't come in. She called and said she was quitting. Even at the end she surprised me. Who in the hell quits on a Monday? I would have thought that Harriet's position was one that just had to be filled, but it wasn't. Rollie and Sarah agreed to parcel the work out between Leah and Anne, and we trundled along as Crispus' book finally got onto the presses.

As a matter of procedure, we notified the authors when their books went into the final phase of production. At the same time we passed along to them for approval art work for the covers of their books. Crispus wired that he would return his sample in person as he was passing through on business.

Rollie thought about that for a time. He usually preferred not having authors anywhere in New York while we were getting their books out, but it didn't really faze him. Rollie would take Crispus to lunch and send him to Radio City Music Hall and that would be that. Nothing really fazed Rollie except losing a contract, and that seldom happened.

I was still backing off job interviews. I was sending out letters and resumés, of course, but I hadn't heard from anyone. I lunched pretty regularly with Lint, and with Obie too, when I could. He was busy on his lunch hours, looking for another job.

A couple of weeks dragged by. I hadn't called Lois, hadn't seen her or Obie. I avoided Lint and Bobbie and stayed pretty much to myself.

Then Obie called me at work.

"Well, man," he said. "I've had it."

"Goddam. Anything in sight? Did you turn up anything?"

"Nothing."

"Do they owe you any money?"

"No, I got all the bread I had coming."

"Obie, you want to move in—"

"Don't be silly, Steve. As much pussy as I get, how can I share a pad with anyone? I'd make you en-vee-ous."

"Cut the clowning, man. What are you going to do?"

"Do? You know I'd better get out there and get my black ass a job. Have you flipped?"

"Obie, why don't you cut out the garbage?"

"Steve, I'm not clowning. Now I can hang out with the—with the—"

"Niggers," I said. Obie couldn't say the word; he hated it.

"Yeah," he said. "Get me a flock of fine broads and put them to work for the old boy, you know? Then I'll get me a contact and start handling high-grade marijuana. Who knows, a month from now I may have a prettier Caddie than Sugar Ray. What color is his?"

"Lavender, I think."

"That's cool. Mine'll be shar-troose!"

"Try to stay in touch, will you, man?"

"But of course, old chap."

"You need any money?"

"I'm fine now," he said, "but please, don't run away."

I laughed. "I'll talk to you in a day or so."

"All right."

I hung up feeling down, way down. I felt for Obie and I was fearful for myself. But for him the grind was on, not *coming* on.

That week looked like a bad one, but toward the end of it I was pleasantly surprised to meet Lois at the bus stop. We climbed on together and stood talking in the aisle. I became conscious of a great strain, just talking to her. Everyone seemed so interested in us. Every time we spoke, heads swung around. And the eyes, the eyes searched, first her, then me as if this was such an impossible thing—a pretty white girl talking without apparent discomfiture, and very familiarly, with a Negro. I suggested we get off about five blocks from our usual stop and walk. She agreed. I felt she was as glad as I to get off the bus.

"You didn't call," she said.

I shrugged.

"I made you an ash tray, best one I ever made, and I wanted you to pick it up, but you didn't call."

I said nothing. It was nice, the walking.

"Do you want some supper?" she asked.

"Are you cooking?"

"Yes."

"Then I'm with you."

Again there was that silence which, between the right people, is more communicative than talking.

"Tell me," I said, "don't you have a boy friend?"

She shook her head without looking at me.

"I can't believe it."

"I've had them," she said. "Let's say I'm between them."

We walked along the park until we got to her place, then we cut in past the doorman. I couldn't resist saying, "What's happening, Dan?"

He glared at me and I smiled. Lois smiled too. She was still smiling when we got into the self-service elevator and the door closed. I kissed her all the way upstairs. When the door opened I knew I was no longer a neuter—a nice guy to be with, a guy who wouldn't touch. And at that point I knew that she didn't want me to be a neuter any longer either.

Holding her hand on the table after dinner, I said with a tight throat, "I'm glad you didn't feel as though I'd rape you."

She removed her hand. "Why did you say that?"

"I don't know."

"I hope you really don't think that, Steve."

"No."

She sipped her wine. I stared at the ash tray she'd made for me. She'd said she designed it to fit my personality, but it really eluded description. I looked up to find her looking at me, not closely but as if she were looking at an object she would begin to paint in a few moments. Her eyes were soft and unblinking. Several times when I thought she might be looking at something else, I turned to find her still looking at me.

"What's the matter?" I asked.

"Nothing," she answered, jerking her head slightly, as if to clear it.

I went to her then and raised her from the chair. She stood poised against my chest, her lips tight against my neck. I don't recall now who was breathing the louder. I whispered into her hair.

"No, Steve," she said, but she didn't mean it, because minutes later I was looking at the melanin spots on her bare back, thinking how the absence of it, almost, made her white and the overwhelming presence of it in my skin made me brown. I left her in bed, a pale nude with sparkling hair. She kissed me lightly and murmured as I left, "Slam the door, dear."

Downstairs I walked slowly along the street. I stifled a desire to cross it and lean on the park wall, to stare into the darkness. I wanted to savor every minute of the past couple of hours. But I went along home. Suddenly I stopped. Something Lois had said was echoing and re-echoing in my brain.

She had said, "I'm glad I met you today. My mother's been on my back all week. I wish I could bring myself to give her a good ringing slap or even shout back at her."

Lois had looked at me then, those gray eyes going wide and deep. "She'd die," Lois said, "if she walked in here and found you nude, in bed with me—nude too."

I started walking home again, only this time I moved slower. You could smell the river, and the winds that blew in from it made the street cool. I was thinking, She hates her mother. She wants to get even with her for the hard times she's caused her, and I'm that tool for revenge. Her mother doesn't really have to know—it's enough for Lois to imagine and delight in her mother's shock.

I didn't think Lois knew what motivated her. Perhaps with the help of her analyst she would soon find out, but until then I had the upper hand. That is, I knew pretty well *why* she saw me.

It had started out a wonderful night. It had ended very messy, and I guess it was fitting that the next day would bring Hadrian Crispus to New York.

Rollie was very gracious with him. He showed Crispus around the office and introduced him to each of us. By now Rollie and I were managing to get along rather stiffly. No one else in the office suspected anything between us, not even Leah, who was pretty sharp. I made a great effort to be pleasant to Crispus. He made no effort to extend his hand, nor did I. If he had to address me, he said, "Hill," not mister. And I, in turn, called him "Crispus." Rollie, I'm sure, was a little amused by it all.

Crispus, like other authors who had come into the office, seemed favorably impressed by the size of it and by the staff. To me it remained a junky place with the covers of books which had been pasted against the walls slipping off and unread manuscripts piled all over hell.

Hadrian Crispus was a big fellow, big and flabby. He had a ruddy complexion and little dull brown spots for eyes. They seemed always slitted against light. His face was that of the rural Southerner, open, pale and without character. His neck was red from the sun and he was uncomfortable in his new white shirt. His hair was flattened down over his head and he had a sweet smell about him, as if he'd been doused with cheap shaving lotion from the five-and-dime. And he had an accent. I've always wondered why it is that Southern whites often have more pronounced accents than Southern Negroes.

I had mixed feelings about this man. He was from Mississippi and as such represented the epitome of Crackerhood; in fact in other sober moods I would have voiced the opinion that the world could get along without him very well. I wanted Rocket to take him for every damned penny he had. But still, a part of me wanted him to escape Rollie's clutches. It was just a small part of me.

Crispus thought he had written a best seller. Can you imagine? His book was about life on the Mississippi Delta. He had some happy, singing Negroes in his book too. They danced also, by the way. Obie had once said that all that dancing that Negroes are supposed to be good at was only aggression disguised. Sometimes I thought Obie a pretty smart guy.

In a way it was fitting that a man like Crispus could not see his work for what it really was, nothing.

I joined Rollie and Crispus. Rollie had it set up so I could preview for Crispus all the publicity and promotion that would take place when his book came out. I laid it on pretty thick, and I suspected Rollie was really getting his jollies underneath.

I couldn't avoid looking closely at Crispus while I was talking. I stood there pretending there was nothing between us, making believe that it wasn't his kind that had jabbed a sprong of a pitchfork through my father's shoulder when he was down in Hinds County with my mother to see me born on the old soil she insisted upon returning to. I remember my father saying how still he was in that pile of hay with all those crackers running around in the goddam dark looking for him because he didn't say "Sir" to one of them. My father said that was when he just forgot about God, because God had forgot about him and let him lie in that stinking hay like an animal. He only kept on going to church because of my mother.

Hadrian Crispus. I looked at him again. Yet he was a man like other men. I recalled that the Germans too were not the killing machines we'd read about, but men. But Crispus hated, and I hated him because I was the target of his hatred and I had done nothing to him. Maybe he hated because he had done it all to me. Consider the fears behind his actions? I couldn't. I could only think of the effect of them.

Southerners are this way to me:

The Germans had left snipers in Viareggio. Not a single street was safe, especially one corner near the edge of town. And the Germans never missed. There had been the usual friction between Negro and white troops, but it was intensified when some Southern boys moved into town. As long as Negro troops were on the street, the white Southern boys walked across that intersection where the snipers never missed. They wouldn't run. They walked as though they were making it through a park or something, and all of us loitered in doorways to watch them. Shaking in their white skins, those crackers stepped from cover. *Bang*! His fellows ran out and dragged him in. Another cracker boy would have to cross the street. He would look from cover to see how many of us were in the doors and windows watching, and when he saw, he would walk out. *Bang*! They would rather die than be afraid in front of a Negro, and we gathered along the walls and in the doors and windows every day to make sure at least a few of them and their Southern pride died.

I guess nothing of what I felt got in the way of my promotion spiel, because when I finished Crispus said, "That's mighty fine, Hill."

"I'm glad you liked it, Crispus."

I left them then. I was a little disgusted with myself—I had a persecution complex, I figured. But was it really a complex, I wondered the next minute, when the things actually were happening to me and to every other Negro in America without letup the moment we stepped into the street each morning? Some of the things were even printed in the daily papers. But the waste was never mentioned—the inexcusable, senseless, horrible waste of lives and talent.

Complex? No.

I was doing all this musing over a milk shake and a ham sandwich. Rollie and Crispus had gone out for lunch, each urging the other through the door first, and Crispus finally going first, his loud voice booming out his thanks. Now Rollie was back.

Rollie shook his head in disgust. "I don't think he's got any money. He kept asking me, 'How much does this cost, how much does that cost?' I sent him off to Radio City. I think he came up here to borrow some money from his brother." Rollie shook his head again.

"Well, we have ours," Sarah reminded him.

"Yes, but that's not all," Rollie said.

"Oh, no?" Sarah said. "He's not coming back to help push the book?"

Rollie began laughing, then said, "Oh, yes!"

Sarah laughed with him, and even Anne, just back from lunch, smiled a little. When the laughter subsided, Rollie said, "I guess we'd better put Steve's plan into operation. How much was that, Steve?"

When Rollie and I had first gone into doing a bit more for our authors, I suggested setting aside a percentage of the total publication charge for use in promotion and publicity. Three per cent was what Rollie had arrived at.

"Two hundred and forty bucks," I said.

Rollie and Sarah looked at one another. Rollie shrugged. They would, I was sure, whittle it down to about a hundred dollars. Some of our authors, the ones who paid nine hundred dollars for a thin little volume of poetry, only got twenty-seven dollars for promotion.

"So much?" Sarah said.

I did something then—I don't know what it was, but it conveyed my disgust for Sarah—and as I went back to my desk, her brown little animal eyes followed me. I'd have to watch it, I realized. Things might get out of control. I'd have to keep real cool.

At the end of the day I went to the john down the hall and came back to the office. Sarah and Rollie must have thought I'd gone for the night—I guess they didn't hear me return. I was staying late to clean up some work. There was a helluva lot of it on my desk. When I finished that, I planned to write to Grace in longhand. It's a nice change when you live all day on a typewriter.

Rollie and Sarah were talking softly. I think they would have lowered their voices if they'd been alone in the middle of the Sahara Desert. I heard my name mentioned. As they went out, Sarah said, "Why give him a raise, Roland? Why? Who else would hire a Negro for a job like this, publicity director?" She grunted. "He likes being dressed when he comes to work, Roland. He is not in the street, a bum. He likes being at a desk with a telephone and a girl to buzz him. Raise? Hah! Put the money in the business. Maybe later you'll give him a raise."

The door closed and they were gone, Sarah's voice echoing the irrefutable truths of an economic trap.

And Rollie, who no doubt had been hoping to get me the raise to ease the stiffness between us, now couldn't.

My appetite was gone and I found I couldn't get any work done. I thought about their voices all the way home, and I imagined what their faces must have been like there in the after-five shadows of the office, in the silence of the building which comes suddenly after about five-fifteen. By the time I arrived home, my face, I felt, was all frozen in a frown, and I knew the moment I walked into my place that I would call Lois.

"Where have you been?" she said.

"Going in early, working late," I said. I felt the need to be curt with her, even to hurt a little. We talked for a long time about her job, her parents, her doctor, the plays and art movies she'd seen. We talked about newspaper and magazine articles and the weather, and when there seemed to be nothing else to say, I said, "I'd like to see you."

"Do you think it wise? We were carried away before."

"I don't care. I want to see you." I waited.

"I have wanted to see you," she blurted out. "I've waited around in the street to see you. I do want to see you, Steve."

"Very much?" I asked.

"Very, very much," she said softly.

Then I said, and I know it sounds crazy, "Second thought. I have something I have to take care of. I'd forgotten it."

"Oh, Steve."

"Sorry," I said, not sure that I really meant it.

"Can't it wait—just a little while?"

"Can't, Lois."

"Will it take long?"

"I'm afraid so."

"Steve, do it tomorrow."

"I can't, Lois. I have to do it now."

"Bastard. You are a bastard."

I hung up. Later I wrote to Grace and as I got ready for bed, I thought back over the conversation with Lois, and I realized I felt better about the miserable day I'd had.

CHAPTER THIRTEEN

I REDOUBLED my efforts to get a decent job. I even went back to the employment agencies. I went to one—I remember it especially because it left me with a helpless feeling—where the interviewer, a dried prune of a woman, said after she looked at my resumé, "You've shifted about terribly, haven't you?"

"Getting experience," I said.

"I see." She looked at me coldly.

"Have you had any difficulty placing Negroes?" I asked. I thought I would give her the chance to say yes and be done with it.

She said, "Heavens, no." She shook her head vigorously. "Only yesterday we placed George Jones. Do you know him?"

I was stunned by the question. There are nearly one million Negroes in New York City. Why in the hell should I know George Jones, any George Jones? I guess because old George Jones was Negro, like me, and we're all supposed to know one another.

"What sort of job did you place him in?" I asked.

"Chauffeur."

Rising, I said, "I take it you don't have anything for me now."

"Let us call you, Mr. Hill. We get so many calls during the day—we'd really prefer you didn't call us."

Then there was the interview on Wall Street. I went down on a lunch hour, certain by the conversation I'd had with the woman on the phone that the job was mine. When I walked in, a woman of about thirty-five snapped, "Why don't you leave the package on the table?"

"I'm not a messenger," I said wearily. "My name's Steve Hill and I have an appointment with Miss Tennet."

"Oh," she said. "You're Mr. Hill."

So I was dead right there and I knew it and she knew it, but the rules say you've got to play the game and we did. She wasn't embarrassed. She stood up and stuck her arm out in the stiff, awkward way women do when they want to give you a man's handshake. We sat down and went through the travesty of the details of the job and salary, and then she said, "We have a few more people to see. Thanks so much for coming."

Another day I stopped to see a girl I'd met through Bobbie. She worked in an employment agency and she said she had something for me. But when I stopped by, she took me into the hall and with a red face told me:

"I was going to tell you the boss got someone else for the job, but that's not right." She took a deep breath. "I asked him not to give this job out because I was saving it for a friend. He asked me about you. Steve, I'm only here because I can't get a part. This is not my life, not this sort of thing. I never knew that—"

"What'd he say, your boss?"

"No dice."

"Why?" I pressed.

"You know why."

"Why did you tell him?"

"I didn't make a point of it, Steve. It just came out." She looked down at the floor. "Why did I have to mention it?"

"Well, for Christ's sake," I said, angrily, "it's not as if I had leprosy. I'm only black."

"I'm sorry," she said.

I cooled down. "Hell, forget it."

"Let's still be friends?" she said. Her name was Maude.

"Sure, Maude. Friends."

I left there. Friend, hell. I don't need anyone for a friend who can for a single second forget what the hell's happening out here or who can pretend for that same second that all's hunky-damn-dory.

I felt way down walking to the subway. Something in me was going up and down. Anger and repression; repression and anger. I stood on the platform, close to the edge, my toes sticking just over the yellow line. You could hear the train rounding a curve. It rocketed nearer, pushing a deadening sound before it. Heat slid swiftly through the tunnel.

For just one vivid second I pictured myself jumping off the platform in front of the train, being ground beneath it, feeling the weight and the heat of it, feeling maybe an arm being ripped off, and a leg, and blood, blood all over the place. Now the train rushed up, a big, black monster. I could see the dim outline of the engineer swaying in the front cabin window. I began to waver. The sound of the train filled everything and seemed to draw me forward. Our eyes met, the engineer's and mine, and his body moved suddenly as I wavered again, then drew back behind the yellow line weak and half faint as the train screeched to a halt, then coasted a few feet forward.

It took me a long time to go to sleep that night.

My fists battered furiously against the brown pine panels. My teeth were grinding so that my jaws ached. I could feel that my face was contorted with anger and frustration. I swung against the pine panels with all my strength and they shattered suddenly and the edges where they had broken loose were stark white. I began to swing again.

And I was still swinging when I woke, tears hot and thick gushing from my eyes. I was crying, "Bastards!" I halted my moving arms with some effort and looked at them. I was surprised. I placed my fingers to my eyes and felt the tears.

"Aw, hell," I said, "Aw, hell." It was what I said when I was a kid when trouble was imminent.

I was glad the next day was Saturday. Perhaps I could work off the uneasy feeling I had by Monday. I got a letter from Grace that day. She said she was coming to see me soon if I didn't stop the foolishness and get back up to Albany to see her. The letter made me feel pretty good. Obie called and wanted to know if we couldn't do something. He sounded discouraged.

When he came in, however, he was restless for some kind of

action. He kept shifting around. We started drinking beer. I played some records. I dug out a weed I'd tucked away after I'd gotten over the cop scare and we blew that while we listened to music. It helped calm him down a little. We talked about women and music, about everything except what was bothering us most. I was still ashamed to tell him about Rollie. I couldn't let him know that I'd been that afraid of losing my job.

Obie patted his stomach. "Let's eat, man."

I staggered up. Another Saturday and high again. "Where?"

"I dunno. Something Spanish."

We went out and got something Spanish, then we stopped in at the Bohemia and caught Art Blakey trying to dominate his group with his snapping, loud beat.

Then we dashed for the "A" train and got off in Harlem. We whizzed in and out of places like two bottles in search of stoppers. Sugar Ray's, the Shalimar.

"The Bandbox!" Obie said. "Let's make it there."

So we did, and after that it was the Red Rooster.

It was in these places that we saw the middle-class Negro. The women, dressed in what Obie called, "High, white fashion." and the men in Ivy League, if they were young enough, or Italian-styled clothing. If it hadn't been for the color of their skins, some of the women, with their red, blonde and streaked hair, might have been taken for sun-tanned white.

Everyone knew Obie when we walked into these places. He was very popular, and you got a good feeling just being with him. As we moved from spot to spot, Obie would point people out to me.

"See that guy? He's cigarettes—Luckies, I think. Over there, that's beer, Knickerbocker—and that real sharp one just in front of the phone booth? That's whiskey—Schenley's." Obie smiled sadly. "Harlem, that's where they work, or when they travel they work in other Harlems in other cities. If there were no Harlems there'd be no them. Wooing the—the—"

"Nigger market?"

"Yes. The Negro market."

I said, "A bitch." I was busy smiling at a coffee-colored blonde.

"Indeed, 'tis indeed," Obie said, clucking.

I was still watching the blonde. I wouldn't have liked Grace with her hair dyed. The blonde stopped smiling at me when a white guy came in, all hip and everything, grinning, and bent and kissed her.

Obie chuckled. "She knows where the money is, man. There isn't a cat in here that can keep her the way this guy does."

"Who is he?"

He laughed again and told me.

Somebody played a Miles Davis side and I listened more to the beat than anything. It was like a heartbeat, thudding ringingly against the cymbals every fourth beat. I watched this white man sit at apparent ease there beside the blonde and I thought, Oh, money and whiteness—just the whiteness gets it.

Obie had grown quiet. We left and walked along the streets, passing small groups of cops on the corners.

"How's it look?" I asked.

We had stopped in an Eighth Avenue bar. It was a dingy, yellow place. Derelicts shambled in and out, their eyes, as they passed you, snapping open in the hope that you'd give them the price of a glass of port, muscatel or thunderbird. Flies whined off the walls; the floor was dirty-white, unevenly set tile. A huge faded refrigerator sat in a corner, and uncovered pans of ribs and chicken parts, cooked, lay in ugly piles on a warmer. We dug our elbows into the top of the bar.

"Nothing," Obie said, "nothing."

I wanted Obie to make out well—a new job, *the* new job—but I wanted one too. I'd feel like hell if he got one and I didn't. Oh, hell, I guess I wanted him to get a good job. I know lots of guys across this country, and Obie, clown that he was, had more on the ball than any ten of them put together. If Obie Robertson couldn't get a job, how could I?

"The thing I hate most," he was saying, "is the grind, the constant looking for something. Then perhaps a little less than what you wanted in the first place, and later just anything." He sighed.

"Thought you were through with compromise."

"I am," he said. "Damned if I'm not through. But lately I've

105

been wondering if my mind and stomach would go along with me."
He pulled hard at his cigarette, and a deep crease ran up and down
in the center of his forehead; the wrinkle was like a knife wound.
"I hate counting pennies and not smoking to save carfare. I hate
going to someone's home at dinner time and being surprised that
it's time for dinner when you're invited to eat."

After a silence I said, "We should have been social workers."

"Now there's security," he said. "All Negroes make good social
workers—they know trouble inside out."

"Or teachers," I said. "I couldn't be a social worker, man. I
couldn't stand anyone else's misery. I got enough of my own."

"We're in the wrong field," Obie said, "or ten years too early."

It was something to think about, but I said, "Aw, Obie, there
you go again."

He smiled. "It's the truth, Steve."

"Nuts."

Obie became suddenly animated. "Ten years from now you still
won't be able to write."

Feigning indignation, I said, "What the hell are you talking
about, man? You never could write copy."

"Steve, my man, you haven't seen the day when you could write
as good as me."

"And layout, Obie. That crap you were doing at *Black*—what
the hell was that supposed to be? Where did you learn *that*?"

"From the same place you did, dammit."

"Let's face it, Obie," I said, turning my back on him, "you can't
touch Steve Hill."

"I'll punch Steve Hill in his goddam mouth," he said, clutching
my shoulder, spinning me around.

I raised my fists and skipped back. "Why? Because he's a better
all-around man than you?"

"No, because he hasn't bought a drink since we've been here,
that's why."

"Drink!" I shouted. All the slumbering drunks darted to their
feet, their eyes flashing up and down and all around, as if a live
one had walked in.

"Go back to sleep!" Obie roared, and we laughed until the tears came.

One bum, a few feet from us, closed his eyes sadly and muttered, "Sumbitches." Obie and I cracked up again.

For a moment we had managed to clown.

Obie took the top off his drink and, staring into his glass, said, "This doesn't get it at all, man."

"No," I agreed.

"A nothing, that's what this is. Saturday night on the town with worries."

I didn't answer. I was thinking of the afternoon and evening, which in a sense had been wasted. In another sense it hadn't. Who could tell? My money was gone and I could have gotten something for Frankie and Teddy. I was irritated with myself for thinking of them.

"I'd like to get out of this country for a while," Obie said. He was high now—that mellow, moody kind of high. That blues high.

"Yeah, me too."

"It'll get worse." He studied me. "Do you know where I would go, my man?"

"My man," I said, "I do not know where you would go."

"To Africa," Obie said with a grand gesture of his arms. "And there, deep in the bush, the lightest thing I'd ever see would be the not so pink soles of my people's feet."

"You don't look at the maps or read papers," I said. "Haven't you ever heard of the *Belgian* Congo, *French* Equatorial Africa, *Spanish* Guinea or *Portuguese* Africa?"

Obie smiled and slapped me on the shoulder. "Kill-joy."

He smiled again, archly; then his face became serious. "Steve. Steve, look here, man. I'm a little high, but I'm all right and you know it, don't you, ol' buddy?"

"Sure, Obie."

"Steve, you know what I'd really like to see?"

"No, man. What?"

"I'd like to see," he said, and his eyes cleared for a second. He looked up over the bar. "I'd like to see the Hercules Brunnen in Colmar."

"Yeah, so would I." We thought about the statue of the Hercules Brunnen with Negroid features in Alsace. It's supposed to have been the thing that sent Schweitzer to Africa.

"Holding up the world as cool as you please," Obie said. "Man, I'd like to see that."

The drone of the flies seemed to fill the place. Obie pushed his hat back on his head. He looked thoughtful. "You know we teach our kids to say, and the old folks say it, that they're proud to be black?"

"Yeah."

"Well, I guess I'm proud to be black too," he said with a hollow laugh, "but I'd like to be white just for a day. One lousy day." He paused. "Steve, do you know something?"

"Sure. You'd be a *bitch* for that day."

"You're abso-goddam-lutely right."

"Must be a great feeling," I said.

"It's unconscious with them. What the hell," he said. "Arise, Negroes, arise. You have nothing to lose but your goddam lives!"

I got us another drink because Obie was getting a little loud. The bums were stirring again. Somewhere in the still night someone began to play a blues record. It went slow and easy; it reached way down and touched a nerve, made it quiver and somehow brought thoughts to your mind. Obie snapped his fingers to the beat—*pap*! *pap*! *pap*! A drunk woke long enough to mutter, "Aw, play it, man!" And we all huddled there listening to the record, the drone of the flies, the police sirens that you hear almost all the time in Harlem. Then the record was over for a minute and the person, some blue person, way up high in a tenement apartment, started to play it again.

Obie said, "I guess I'll call Gloria to come and get me." He smiled. "It's good for my ego, you know." He started to the phone booth and stopped and turned to me. "What is it that ties us so inexplicably to women?"

I started to say something wise.

"No, it's more than that," he said, as if he'd read my mind.

"Then I don't know. Maybe we still need mothers."

108

"Yeah, maybe that's it. Hey, you ever feel incestuous?"

The question startled me because at the moment I was thinking of Grace. I still had some guilt feelings about her having been married to my brother. "No," I said.

Obie went to the booth. He left the door open, and above the sound of the blues, the drone of the flies and the police sirens, I heard him say, "Baby, baby, please come and get me." Then he told her where he was.

I waited with him until Gloria came. His eyes lighted up the moment she came through the door; so did hers, and I have seldom in my life felt as alone as I did the moment they rushed up to each other and embraced. A drunk opened one eye and peeked at Gloria's legs, then he closed it and went back to sleep with a little smile on his face. Obie and Gloria turned and walked slowly into the street.

I had one more drink. I drank it slowly and listened to that record that was being played all over again and I tried to think of the kind of blues the person who played it had. Lonely blues? Woman blues? Or just plain old inescapable nigger blues?

I caught a cab and got out a few blocks from home. I wanted to walk. I saw clouds scudding across the sky, looking as if they would run into the buildings; then miraculously they were past, racing northward, and the bright, early morning sky broke out, a single, blazing star spearheading it from the east. One newsstand was open, its incandescent lights blaring soundlessly into the street. I bought a *Times* at the stand and, tucking it under my arm, thrusting my hands deep into my pockets, I decided I liked New York like this, just before dawn; just before people poured out of and into offices; before the noises started screaming through the glass-brick, asphalt-floored canyons; before the light came up and the buildings became harsh and their windows glinted like the points of steel daggers. At that moment New York was mine and I was surveying it, sauntering through it, making sure everything and everyone in it was all right.

I wished I could call someone and say, "Baby, please come get me." I thought suddenly of Grace then, and her letter, and I didn't feel so alone, so blue.

CHAPTER FOURTEEN

THE TELEPHONE woke me. My head was a little big.

At least, *I* called her at decent hours, I thought. It *was* Lois.

"You going to sleep all day?"

"What time is it?"

"Four o'clock and it's beautiful out."

"Already?"

"Who did you sleep with last night?" She laughed when she asked it—an embarrassed laugh.

"I didn't."

"You weren't home all night."

"You've been calling," I said, pleased.

"Oh, a couple of times. Got a hangover?"

"How did you guess? Want to come down and fix coffee?"

There was a pause. "Just coffee? Well, I did want to talk with you . . ."

"Just coffee," I assured her.

I let her in when she came, then I crawled back into bed. She sat looking sad while the coffee perked. Finally she said, "You must have got some load on last night."

I grunted.

"Who were you with?" She had an odd, fixed smile on her face. There was something in her questions that irritated me.

"Guy I went to school with. Why?"

"Just wondered. Want to take a shower?"

I nodded ever so gently. "What was it," I asked, "that you wanted to talk about?"

"Later," she said. "Want a clean towel?"

"No. That one's all right."

She turned the shower on. "Ready in five minutes," she said. I heard the refrigerator door open. "What are you going to eat for dinner? You don't have a damned thing in the box."

"Going out," I muttered.

"I'll cook—if you'll buy groceries."

"Okay. Take the five on the dresser."

She took it and went out, humming. I felt better by the time she got back with something like seven cents change. "You said just coffee," I reminded her. "Now you want to make dinner."

"You know what I meant," she said, with mock menace. She took a swipe at me.

"Is that what you wanted to talk about?"

She nodded.

"Don't you have anything to drink?" she asked.

I looked at her. I had half a flask of Scotch. I got it and gave it to her.

"Three drinks," she said. "Not bad. You've had yours."

I waved a hand in bitter agreement as she poured herself a drink.

"Idiot," she said softly. "What do you see in getting drunk?"

"That's why I do it—so I won't have to see anything."

She smiled, but deep behind it there was sadness.

When dinner was ready, I got out some candles and lighted them. There was a bit of Chianti left and I brought it out. Then I put some records on the phonograph.

"Eat," Lois said.

Outside it was beginning to get dark. Lois, inside with me, was very beautiful in the candlelight, with its flames sparking highlights from her hair. Her eyes seemed impossibly soft and I kept asking myself, What am I doing here with this beautiful woman?

"Want to talk now?" I asked.

"I don't want to see you anymore," she said.

I kept eating.

"That's not right, Steve. I *can't* see you anymore."

I continued eating.

"You know why. But I love you, I think, very much."

"No problem then," I said.

"It *is* a problem." She put down her fork. "I'm not hungry anymore."

"How's it with the doctor?"

She sipped her wine, looked at me, eyes widening, softening. "We talk about you at almost every session. I dreamed about you twice last week."

"Tell me about the dreams."

"I only remember one."

I took her hand. "Go on. Tell me."

"It's very short."

"Tell me, baby."

"Someone," she said, tracing her fingers lightly over my hand, "had been cruel to you at your office. You jumped out the window."

"What!" I was thinking about the thirty-floor drop to 42nd Street.

Lois shrugged. "I couldn't help it. I dreamed it."

"Well, don't dream anymore."

She snickered.

Dinner was over. We stacked the dishes in the sink and I got Lois to stay, though she wanted to leave right then. We sprawled out on the floor. And talked.

"This thing—it's happening so fast," she said. She looked at me. "And I'm afraid."

I rolled over. "Baby," I said. "I wouldn't have you be afraid for anything in this world. So why don't you run along and we'll forget it."

"Don't be like that, dear," she said, kissing me. I held her just a little off.

"You're getting moody," she said, "and bitter."

"No, I'm just thinking."

I couldn't hold her off. She rested her head on my chest. "You are so nice, Steve. I've become so used to you—to hearing your voice on the phone. When you're not home when I call, I'm just so on edge. I shouldn't be like this and I don't want to be." She sighed. "But when we're like this, it all seems so—so perfect."

My heart surged. "I don't want you to go," I said.

"I'd better."

"No."

"You want me to stay?"

"Yes, I do."

"I don't know what to say—right after my noble speech. I've been practicing it for days—even when I was out on dates I never enjoy anymore for thinking about you, and wondering who you're with. What should I say?"

"Say yes."

"Steve?"

"Yes, doll?"

"I don't know what to *say*."

"Say yes."

She nestled her head tightly against me and nodded it. I wanted then to place my arms gently around her, but I didn't. I just lay there thinking.

"Sometimes," she said, her voice very tiny, very lovely, "when I'm with you, I have nothing my own. If I have, it's for you."

And then I placed my arms around her and drew her to me.

But she was not going to see me after that, she said, but I didn't have the feeling she meant it.

The next evening I couldn't stay in the apartment that Lois had filled so wonderfully the night before. Without calling, I walked to Lint's. I just wanted to sit with company. When I got upstairs, Lint stared at me in surprise.

"What's the matter with you?" I asked.

"Didn't—" He began to choke. "Uh—Bobbie was—" He finally stopped and began over again. "This is a little upsetting," he said. "Bobbie said she was going to the store and then drop over to your place and bring you back for supper." He turned away from me. I knew he was very hurt. "You didn't see her, huh?"

"No," I said, wishing to hell I'd called or, better still, had not budged from my apartment. I started to go.

"Stick around," Lint said. "It's not your fault."

"Man, I'm really sorry."

"What the hell," he said. "I've been suspecting it for a long time."

I said nothing. I wanted out of there.

We watched some TV for about ten minutes. Then there was the sound of a key in the door. Bobbie walked in.

"Steve!" she said. "You bastard. I was just over to your place and left a note in the door. Was going to bring you over here for dinner."

She paused and looked at us. I broke out in a big grin. Lint turned away and I could see his body heave with relief.

"What the hell is the matter?" Bobbie asked.

"Nothing," Lint said. "Steve and I were just having one of our serious conversations."

"C'mon," she said. "Drinks first, dinner next. Fix your own. Here's the liquor."

She dashed into the kitchen. Lint and I avoided looking at one another. During dinner Bobbie again reminded me of Lois. Odd that they seemed to move the same way and had practically the same mannerisms. Afterward, we watched the shows in silence except when Bobbie called off the names of some of the actors she knew. At least two shows came on for which she'd auditioned. She snarled at the actresses who'd got the parts.

"That bitch!" she ranted. "Oh, what a slut!"

Lint looked at me and raised his hands, palms upwards in a gesture of helplessness. In a way his gesture was more than that. It indicated his inability to cope with his wife and I wondered if he had ever been able to handle her. Bobbie burst into tears.

"Honey," he said, going to her.

"Get away!" she snarled. There was a wicked flash of hatred in her eyes as she retreated like an animal from him. I knew Lint wished I wasn't there to witness it. "I'm going for a walk," she said. She ran to the closet and snatched a sweater and flew out the door, slamming it behind her.

"Man," Lint said when she'd gone. "Damned if I know what to do. She starts crying when she sees kids she knows on television or when she reads the Sunday *Times* and sees where someone else got a good part. Christ! I spend all my time cheering her up. I don't have any guarantee that I'll be a success as a writer. My future's in worse shape than hers, dammit!"

He wanted to talk it out. I didn't say anything.

"What am I supposed to do?"

"I suppose," I said, "you'll have to see it through."

"Yeah, well, I'm getting damned sick and tired of seeing it through. Man, just a few months of the old days—a bottle of beer, reams and reams of paper and a typewriter in a cold water flat. How that appeals to me!"

"You've lost your Bohemian tastes, old man."

"I have like hell." He broke off abruptly and said, without looking at me, "Call me tomorrow at work. Tell me if there's a note at your place."

Then he looked at me, and I looked at him. "Sure," I said.

"What's the answer, Steve?" He was going back to what he had been talking about before.

Irritated, I said, "Man, don't ask me what the goddam answer is. How the hell should I know?"

He flushed.

I couldn't tell whether he was sneering or straight-talking when he said, "Don't be smug just because you've got your problems prepacked in your color."

"I got to go," I said.

"Don't forget the note."

"How could I?"

He flushed again and I went downstairs and ran into Bobbie. She was still crying angrily. She said, "Can I walk with you? You must be awfully sick of us by now."

"Sure, walk with me. You know the spiritual, 'Walk with me, Jesus'?"

She smiled and blew her nose. "No."

"Neither do I."

"Steve?"

"What, doll?"

"Lint—Lint got me into trouble with a director."

"What do you mean?"

She started to sniffle again as we walked up the street.

"I got a call for a show. My first Broadway thing. I did very well the first two rehearsals. I talk with Lint about everything, you know, and I told him what the director had me do with the part.

He said I should stand up to him and tell him he was doing it all wrong. It sounded logical, Steve, what Lint said, so the very next day I told the director he was doing it wrong and he very acidly told me why he was doing it his way, and that sounded right, Steve, absolutely right. He canned me that very day. Lint was sympathetic, but I think he was really very happy. Do you know that? Actually happy."

It was Bobbie's turn to talk it out and I remained silent.

"Do you know what I think it is, Steve?"

"What?"

"I just cannot become a success before he does. He's got to be first."

"I don't believe that," I said, but I did.

"It's the truth. God, how can we go on this way?"

"Bobbie," I said finally, "is there a note for me? Did you leave one?"

We walked a few paces before she answered. "He asked you to let him know, didn't he?"

I nodded.

"There's no note, Steve."

"Bobbie!" A voice called then, and out of the crowds, half walking, half sprinting, came a young, handsome guy whom I recognized as an off-Broadway director who was coming up fast. He only had eyes for Bobbie. Perhaps, like so many people, he refused to accept the fact that we were walking together because I was black; that just could not be the case. His eyes clouded for just one second when Bobbie touched me on the arm and excused herself.

"I'll be right back," she said. Her eyes were shining too. Maybe this guy was the one she'd left not too long ago. He reached possessively for her arm as she went toward him. Bobbie looked backwards at me and withdrew it timidly. The eyes of the man shot toward me. Now Bobbie was talking to him and he relaxed.

My move was clear. I left them and walked on home.

When I called Lint at his office the next day, I cheerfully told him that there was a note, and I read one I'd made up, but he only grunted and hung up.

CHAPTER FIFTEEN

*H*E DIDN'T believe me, and when he hung up the way he did, I knew he was almost past believing anything. I couldn't say that I felt very sorry for him.

The following weeks I was busy preparing copy for the Christmas season. *O, Come Ye Back* was about to come off press, and there was the New York deal Rollie told me to see about—radio, television and whatever else we could get.

I had little time, even if I had wanted it for worrying about Lint and Bobbie. I didn't call Lois and I didn't see her. I was taking the subway to work early and getting home late. She called two or three times and we talked briefly. I had the feeling when she called that it was to give me the opportunity to ask to see her. I didn't.

Obie had moved. To where, I didn't know—he just upped and left his old place. I didn't know his girl's last name or I would have called there. I had to wait for him to call me.

And Grace was still on my neck to come up to Albany.

O, Come Ye Back was one of the few Rocket books that came out on schedule. We earmarked for Crispus his seventy-five author copies, free of charge. I managed to get some radio time on a couple of local stations. I wrote releases for consumption near Crispus' home. I contacted farmer groups.

The approach I used was integration. Everyone was interested in it, of course, but Crispus had nothing about it in his book. If anything, he was for the status quo, him and his goddam happy darkies. But you always need a hook and that was the one I chose, phony as it was.

Hadrian Crispus also wanted a reception—to start off the promotion. Rollie tried to talk him out of it, long distance, but was unable to do so. He would have tipped his hand had he pressed. So I set up a reception for Crispus at one of the small, East Side hotels. I sent letters (probably the best I ever wrote) to the book editors of *Life-Time*, *Newsweek*, the *Times*, the *Tribune* and a dozen other publications.

There must have been very little promotion before I arrived at Rocket. Had there been, these people would have known us a little better and would not have responded the way they did.

The faith of a Mississippi Delta farmer and its application to today's integration crisis. That's what I'd said. You only have to mention Integration and Mississippi in one breath and people stop, look, and don't quite believe it.

There's not too much difference between integration violence and any other form of violence; people rush to look.

I listed the names of the people who would be attending the reception from their responses by mail and phone. I sent them follow-up telegrams and then secured telephone confirmation of their attendance. Through some good luck I met, through a friend, a television personality on the way up. He agreed to come to the reception and have Crispus on his show for a minute or so, coast-to-coast. I swung some lesser people into coming for the decorations, and the affair was set, complete with photographer, when Crispus arrived in town.

He raved about his book. There was something pitiful about the way he picked it up, hefted it, smelled the newness of it.

"Mr. Culver," he told Rollie, "I don't believe there's ever been a better-looking book than mine." He patted it proudly. We were smiling, of course, and making enthusiastic little chitchat.

"Mr. Crispus," Rollie said, "that's one of the best jobs we've ever done. Even I was surprised. I guess the entire staff was inspired by the great work you did yourself."

Crispus grinned. He leaned forward, cuddling the book beneath his arm. "Confidentially," he said, "it took all my savings—and you know what happened the last time I was here?"

"Yes?" Rollie said. He didn't bat an eyelash.

"I went to see my brother so I could go ahead plannin' things for next year if I got some money from him?"

Southerners have a way of making statements sound like questions.

"Yes?" Rollie said. I noticed that his voice had risen in pitch to match Crispus'.

Crispus laughed. "He called me a fool an' wouldn't give it to me, but"—he laughed heartily—"wait until he gets a look at this." Crispus stroked the book. "It's going to make me a pile of money," he said. "I just know it."

"Not a pile," Rollie said with a smile. "Maybe half a pile."

Crispus laughed again. "Mr. Culver, you sure do like to joke."

Sarah winked at Crispus. "He's the only one in the office who has time enough to joke," she said with a friendly smile. "He's the boss."

"Has there been much advance sale?" Crispus asked.

"Things are shaping up nicely," Rollie said. His smile was big, open and, to Crispus, honest.

The answer seemed to satisfy the farmer. There had not been a single advance sale, of course. Crispus then gave me a list of his friends in Texas, California and Mississippi who would buy copies. I put the list on my desk. It was damned hard for me to believe that Crispus truthfully thought he had a big thing with his book, but he did. I kept wondering when he would wake up. He gave us the name and number of his hotel, saying, as he left, that he would be available any time for lectures and interviews. Rollie told him that things probably would not be moving much until after the reception. Crispus said, with a big wink, "I'm sure they'll move all right."

Rollie had cut down on the promotion percentage for Crispus' reception, but the money was still pretty nice in comparison with the nothing I'd had to work with before. I was able to set the thing up so that it appeared solid anyway.

Early in the afternoon, before the reception got underway, I checked food and drinks at the hotel and got Charlie, the photographer, to follow me around and take pictures at a signal from me. I wanted him to get his pictures quickly because it figured that as soon as the guests got in, they'd smell a hoax and leave in a hurry.

A guy from the *Saturday Review* came in. I grabbed Crispus, who had come in only seconds after me, not wanting to miss anything, and steered him close to the *SR* man. I nodded and Charlie took a picture. The *SR* man looked around startled. I walked away. People were coming in steadily now, and a little cautiously. Crispus and I walked around introducing ourselves. Charlie was right behind us, busy with his camera. Once I heard Rollie say, "I'm Roland Culver. I'm the president of Rocket." Someone mumbled, "Nice to know you."

The television personality came in and Crispus recognized him. When they were introduced, Crispus said, "You mean I'm going to be on a show with you? A television show?"

The television personality looked from Crispus to me, and I imagine he was trying to discover who was responsible for this farce. He walked away with Crispus trailing him.

The dead horse was being scented. I could see people merging together, whispering. But the food and drinks were free and they lingered. Some of the guests spoke with me about my job. They seemed curious and appeared to be thinking that Rocket couldn't be such a bad outfit to have a Negro publicity man.

Finally the crowd began to thin. I could see some of the guests going out with grins on their faces, whether for themselves or for the farce Rocket had just put on, I couldn't tell. I rescued the television personality from Crispus and he rushed out. From the way Rollie was grinning, I knew we'd had a great success.

We would use the pictures for the next brochure going to prospective authors; they would be a selling point. The pictures would show Crispus chatting amiably with New York's book people, the implication being that the book was a good one and these people had rushed to congratulate the author. And perhaps we would also use the photographs for the newspapers in or near Crispus' home.

I could not get an autograph party for Crispus in New York. He finished his radio spots and hung around until he had his television show. Then Rollie sent him packing home, having assured him that there, too, we had made arrangements for radio and television appearances and many autograph parties. Crispus left, promising to return if we needed him, and we all heaved a sigh of relief. You could feel the tension relaxing with the approach of the holidays.

"What a pain in the ass *he* was," Sarah said, when Crispus had been gone a couple of days.

I could not help thinking how very much Sarah sounded as if it were her right to con and insult people, and that if they somehow obstructed her in the routine performance of that operation, *they* were bothersome little swindlers. Then I thought of Crispus getting off the train in Jump-off, Mississippi, or some other damned hole, holding his book high, waving it and crying to the cotton-picking world to look at his dream come true.

I could not decide whether I was glad it had happened to him or sorry, and that is the truth.

CHAPTER SIXTEEN

A DAY OR so before Thanksgiving I sat moping at my desk trying to look busy and trying not to feel sorry for myself. Leah came in. She stood looking out the window and I sat shifting papers from the top of a pile to the bottom. I turned to her.

"Why don't you get out of this?"

She shrugged. "As soon as I get married. I don't want a career, I just want a home and children. There's no point in my running from job to job."

We watched Anne flounce around. Leah said, "Poor kid. She thinks this is such a big deal."

"Yeah, I guess so."

Anne and Sarah became engaged in an earnest conversation.

"You having any luck?" Leah asked. She knew I was looking for something else.

"No."

"Steve, that's awful. Gee, I'll keep looking and listening."

"Thanks. That's sweet."

"So are you, Steve, and I wish you'd get some luck. By the way, old boy, when are you getting married?"

"I don't know," I said. A chill hit me. I was thinking of Lois instead of Grace.

"Soon?" she went on.

"I don't know," I laughed. "Beat it. Earn your money."

She went out laughing. Then and there I decided to call Lois that evening. I did, and she came down.

She didn't say anything for a long time. She just sat looking at me, and looking at the floor. Finally she said, "I've wanted so much to see you."

"Have you?"

"Yes."

We didn't talk for about five minutes, then she said, "How weak I am. How very weak."

"For coming down?"

"No."

"What then?"

"You know, don't you?"

I didn't say anything.

"It isn't right for me to love you. My parents would die. Don't I owe them something?" She went on, not giving me a chance to answer. "Yet, it seems I have to be near you or talk to you. I keep wondering why—we know each other such a short time."

"But you're here," I said, not saying what I should have said.

"Yes," she said. She looked directly at me. "For the last time."

"You've said that before."

She clasped her hands across her face. "I know. Each time I say it, I mean it, Steve. I do mean it."

"Do you?"

She nodded. Then she changed the subject. "How's the job hunt going?"

I had told her about it. "Nothing," I said.

"That's another thing," she said. "If you weren't Negro you'd have no problem getting a job. I guess in a way I'm like all those people who say 'no' to you every day."

I looked at her and I felt a little frightened, just the way I felt when I was a kid playing hide-and-go-seek and the searcher drew near my hiding place.

"I want to take you to a party," I said.

"When?"

"Saturday."

"But—"

"Saturday."

She looked at me a long time. "All right."

Later, as we were smoking, and after I had put her into stitches talking about Crispus, she said, "I dreamed about you a couple of nights ago."

"Tell me." I got my curiosity from dreams naturally. My father used to knock me out with his dreambook. Dream of snakes and look up snakes in one of those books and play the number opposite it. I still remember it—536.

"Your office staff was having a party somewhere," she said. "I walked in and everyone was surprised to see me go toward you. I was a stranger—and to be heading straight for you with that look in my eyes you tell me I always have . . ." She passed me her cigarette. "I sat down," she continued, "beside you, and I was very attentive, touching you and so on. You were a little embarrassed, I think, the way you can be sometimes." She paused to kiss me. "Everyone looked, but I didn't give a damn because I wanted to be with you, no matter what. It seemed as if I had not seen you in a long time. Later the party broke up. We had caught each other's eye and it was understood that we would meet outside and go somewhere. You left first and I left shortly after.

"As I came out I could see you walking rather fast, and this surprised me. It was as if you were trying to leave me, go away from me. You went into some kind of forest and I went running after you. I saw a trail that curved over a hill and I was quite positive you'd taken it, so I followed it. Overhead, for some reason, there was a tiger. It stalked back and forth. At first I was very afraid, but when I saw it made no move to attack, I ran on and voices came to me saying, 'Watch out for the tiger, watch out for the tiger.'

"You were nowhere in sight when I got to the top of the hill. Then I heard a lion roar, and I saw two of them mauling something in the grass and for a minute my whole being was wrapped up in the thought of how it would feel to be torn limb from limb. But I went on looking for you. I didn't find you."

I tried not to expel my breath too quickly or too loudly. "What did your doctor say?"

"He helped me with parts of it."

"What was in the grass?"

"I don't know. I didn't get that close. I had a powerful feeling that it wasn't you."

"The voices?"

"Consciences, Steve. Yours, mine, society's."

"Nuts. And you never did find me?"

"No."

"Sure?"

She looked at me, puzzled. "Yes, I'm sure. Why?"

"Nothing." I sighed. "Most colorful dream I've heard described."

"Most colorful one I've ever *had*. There was no twin feature, I'm not sorry to say."

We were silent thinking about the dream.

"Why did you ask if I was sure I hadn't found you in the dream?"

"The tiger," I said.

"The tiger?"

"Wasn't I the tiger?"

She thought a moment. "I don't get the connection," she said.

"Well, it wasn't anything."

"Do you think you were the tiger?"

"Yes."

"Why?"

I shrugged. "Just a hunch. Can't explain."

If I had explained, she would have had the picture I wasn't ready for her to have. A tiger is a violent animal—a predatory beast that likes warm blood. She had pictured a tiger without violence, which did not mean, of course, that the violence wasn't present. Again I had the feeling of near discovery. I was uneasy with myself for showing her only parts of the portrait.

"Lois?"

"Yes, dear?"

"After Saturday—after Saturday, let's quit it."

I could almost hear silence moving in the room.

She said, "Why does it sound so horrible when you say it?"

For a week then, as if we were to die at the end of it, Lois and I saw each other. It was only because of her that I could look with some humor at the job situation. She was more than fun; she seemed to be everything. It was during that week that I began to think a little about us. To think at length about it was to look at evil. I only thought about it, as I said, a little.

We went to the uptown movies and saw a couple of off-Broadway things. We seemed to have agreed, without saying it, that we would try to stay away from crowds. That Saturday we went to a small party in Yorkville. We would have had a nicer time if we hadn't been so busy thinking we wouldn't see each other again. When the party was over, we walked a little ways before hailing a cab. We strolled around looking at the harsh contrasts of svelte modern buildings pimpled with air conditioners standing between drab, scarred tenements. We looked at the scenery beyond the East River and decided the view we had over the Hudson to New Jersey was infinitely better. It was about two when we began walking west, swinging our hands between us.

We waited for the light to change at First Avenue. Across the street, a small group of men came out of a dull, poorly lighted bar. In an instant the air seemed charged with tension. I don't know if Lois had noticed it or not. The light changed and we walked across the street, approaching the group. Other men crowded into the door of the bar behind them. They made motions to each other, spoke quickly, quietly.

My stomach began to hammer and fear gripped it suddenly with strong fingers. We were abreast, and then past them. I heard footfalls on the concrete behind us. They were quick, running, then they stopped. Lois was saying something, but I wasn't listening. I was watching our shadows, tall before us, from the street light behind us. If other shadows suddenly leaped into view—

"You lousy slut, you no-good bitch!"

A two-by-four rattled past us and bounced off a car.

"You! Why don't you go back where you came from, nigger?"

Part of a brick skidded past us on the walk, crumbled into fast-moving tiny pieces.

"Tramp! White trash! Get back in the gutter where you belong!"

Lois leaped forward as though she'd been struck in the back with a heavy object. "Is that for *us*?" she asked. She didn't believe it. She began to shudder.

"I'm afraid so, doll."

She began to walk faster. She gripped my hand tighter.

"Steve, I'm afraid."

I looked around for a cop. None there, of course. They were all up in Harlem. "Lois, listen to me. I'm afraid, too—you'll never know how afraid—but don't run. That'll get 'em started."

She nodded. Her face was pale and her eyes wide, but she didn't once break stride. We kept sauntering along, holding hands, swinging them. It was our little way of showing defiance.

"Whore!"

"Go, black boy, go!"

"Tramp, tramp, dirty, stinkin' tramp!"

Finally we were at Second Avenue. It had been the longest block I'd ever walked in my life. I took a deep breath and looked very hard at her. I knew anger so thick, so hot, that I began to choke on it. I wanted a cab to come quickly. When it did, squealing into our silence, I put Lois in and closed the door.

"Steve! Wait! Where are you going? What are you going to do?"

"Go back. I *have* to go back."

"No, no, Steve, please get in. There are too many of them. If you don't get in, I'll go back with you!" She clutched at the door. I held it firmly closed.

"Take her home," I told the driver. "She's drunk." The cabbie started up. "If I'm not home in an hour, call the cops," I said to Lois. But the cab was already moving. The white cabbie probably figured that if his passenger was drunk she had no business with me.

God, I didn't want to go back. I had to. I started back down the block. It had nothing to do with heroics, not even honor, whatever the hell that may be. A little man sat inside my chest beating a tom-tom. I looked for a brick, a stick, anything; a bottle maybe.

I walked quickly down the street. I didn't want a part of me to talk the other part of me out of it. Anger flowed up to join the fear. They had frightened the hell out of me and that intensified my anger. I was angry mostly because the last place I might have a few moments peace when I left my house were the streets, and now even they were going and, goddamit, I had to fight for the right to share that last, garbage-strewn place, because after that, man, they'd be right inside your damned door asking you out.

The cries of that mob slamming hard off the walls of the empty street, I thought as I approached the corner, were the audible messages many eyes flashed when Lois and I were together. The mob, the animals. They had risen from the inanimate viciousness of a Reginald Marsh painting, had crowded together to give strength to each, and had howled out into the street as beer-sodden hyenas. You kill hyenas.

I saw nothing in the street I could use for a weapon, but it didn't matter. I wanted to feel flesh pressed tightly between my thumbs, feel skin roll beneath the pressure of them. I wanted to duck a lunge, snatch the feet of the lunger and, spinning, hurl him into the path of an oncoming car. I wanted to drive my fist out of my arm, out of my elbow, out of my shoulder and to hell with massive retaliation.

They were gone. All of them gone.

I didn't go into the saloon. As angry as I was, I remembered where the cops could tie you up. The bartender would claim I went in looking for trouble and I would have had it.

I stood there on the corner a minute or two, feeling relief, disappointment and confusion. A young, thin cop strode by, bouncing his stick from the end of its thong. He looked at me; he looked at me hard. I walked out into the street and caught a cab before he thought up something.

In the cab I wondered why they were so rough on Lois. Was it because she too was white and had apparently deserted them for me? I didn't know. All the way home I looked at the back of the cabbie's head and neck. They were white, and I didn't want to see anything white. Nothing. So I was surprised to find Lois waiting outside my building.

"I'm glad you're here. What happened?"

"Nothing. They were gone. How do you feel?"

"A little nervous. You?"

"Uh—like I'd been hit."

"Shall we go upstairs?"

I didn't want her to come up. "No. I'm going right to bed.

She was surprised, but she composed herself and changed the subject. "Was that the first time something like that has happened to you?"

"Yes." I started up the stairs.

"Please, Steve, let me go upstairs with you."

"No, Lois. This is Saturday, the end." And I meant it.

"I know, dear, but this—Oh, it was so horrible." She put her hand to my face. She rubbed it tenderly but it inflamed me.

"It won't come off," I said.

She jerked her hand away, but only to give me a stinging slap. In a flash I was on the balls of my feet, my arm half-cocked. Then I halted, wavered a little. If I'd hit her, she would have known what she had almost discovered a couple of times before.

She said, as tears came to her eyes, "I don't understand why you want to hurt me so much, Steve."

She turned, then, and walked down the street toward her home. She looked very tiny in the dark with her shoulders hunched way up. I could tell she was crying.

Upstairs, I felt an overwhelming urge to shower. When I finished,

I lay in bed smoking and thinking. "I'll go back with you," she had said.

I sat up in bed, suddenly feeling very sick, very ashamed, but all the same, when the phone rang, I didn't answer it. I knew it was Lois.

CHAPTER SEVENTEEN

LETTERS—dozens of them—began to pour in from Crispus. What had happened? What was happening? What was going to happen? The book seller in his home town had sold twenty-five copies of *O, Come Ye Back*, but he hoped when he got his financial statement from us we'd have sold five hundred times that.

But we hadn't.

Each letter during those first two weeks in December was filled with bewilderment and hurt. I answered his letters although they were addressed to Rollie. I signed Rollie's name. I was pouring over one of Crispus' letters one day when Obie walked in, thin and tired-looking.

"Where in the hell have you been?" I asked.

"You know." His voice didn't seem as powerful as usual. "The grind."

"I'm going down to the warehouse," I said. "Come with me."

"Sure," he said. "I don't have anything to do."

"We'll grab lunch later."

"Fine. You buying?"

"If you, buy with your first pay check."

"It's a deal."

Obie was as quiet as a shadow as we walked through the warehouse. I looked at people's dreams stacked there from floor to ceiling. Books. Their trite titles peered outwards. Poetry, religion, adventure, how-to, fiction, biographies—all sad and corpselike. I walked slowly through the piles of books. It was like a mausoleum.

This was the light of day Rollie talked about. It was profitable for a vanity house to allow its books only the light of day of this sort. The real money, the only money, was made in printing and printing alone. Shipping and selling only entailed paper work, additional help and expenditures. If a book, by some freak of nature, began to sell, it would then become to the printers an unprofitable book, especially if the number sold exceeded the number originally printed. Then the presses, if this happened, would have to be set up all over again or the entire book photo-offset, and either method costs the printer money. But the authors didn't know this.

And they didn't know that a sixty-four page book ran them a bit over five hundred dollars, actual cost for labor and manufacturing—and that four to five hundred dollars, if the subsidy was nine hundred or a thousand, went in clear profit to the printer.

Nor did they know that the greatest cost was in composition. A sixty-four page book cost about one hundred fifty dollars to set up, a five-hundred-page book about fifteen hundred. The press work ranged from seventy to over ninety dollars, depending upon the size of the book. Paper ran about four cents per sheet and jacket art about one hundred dollars. Binding charges started at about ninety and went up to two hundred and thirty-five dollars.

There were few markets for vanity books. Book sellers wouldn't take them, and only ordered them upon the request of a customer. Most publicity outlets were closed except in the small and medium-sized towns. The only discernible vanity book market was the author's circle of friends, his true friends, and one seldom has two hundred and fifty true friends.

Two hundred and fifty printed and bound books was the maximum for a vanity house, although the contracts—neat, official, gold-sealed things—usually called for editions of perhaps twelve hundred. The basic run was a printing of five hundred and binding of two hundred and fifty. The vanity publisher, like Rocket, could always say that, like regular publishers, they did not bind the entire edition at once. It was very rare, however, for a vanity publisher to be placed in a position like that.

I saw Crispus' books in the storehouse. There were ninety there. He had received seventy-five, twenty-five had been sold, and I had sent out sixty to reviewers on small Southern newspapers, mostly in Mississippi. We always sent out books to reviewers, then we could always list the papers to which they were sent for the author, if he demanded it. We then could say, when a book was not doing well, which was usual, "Is it our fault that the reviewer didn't like it?"

"Obie," I said, "let's get out of here."

"All right. I'm hungry."

At lunch I asked Obie where he was staying. He wouldn't tell me. He wouldn't give me Gloria's last name either.

"Obie, what the hell's the matter, man?"

"Steve, when I get squared away, everything will be like it used to be. But now, with me on the skids, I don't want help, I don't want sympathy, and I'm sick of handouts."

"Jesus, man, you'd do the same for me."

"I got to do it my way, Steve. Try to understand, will you?"

"I understand."

"Sure?"

"You know I understand."

"I have to go now," he said abruptly.

"Obie," I said, getting up, "don't rush off like this. When will I see you again?"

He tried to grin. "I'll drop around, Steve." He walked off, but stopped. "Don't worry, man, and thanks."

"Sure."

I sat down to finish my coffee feeling for him. From his point of view, he, Obie, was the world—nothing existed without him. He could not be helped out. In his world, *he* helped people without fanfare, without being Christlike, because it was the thing to do if it had to be done. His faith was great—maybe the only way to have it, if you must—and I dreaded the day when Obie finally would lose that faith. For Obie knew that once the world's people ceased to barter in skills and human values, once it concentrated on eradicating, by whatever means, people with color, just because they had it, his was a world destroyed. Obie believed in his world much more than he had a right to, maybe, but you have to believe in something until it's all gone, every mosquito's pee-drop of it. And that's just about where Obie was—down to the last drop.

I could understand his wanting to be out of sight. It hadn't been too long ago when I had wanted to keep out of my brother's sight—away from his solicitousness, from his kindness and pity. All I had then, like Obie now, was the desire to have some pride.

I was still thinking about it when I stopped at a new employment agency to keep an appointment. The receptionist let me in to see the director right away. He was a pleasant-looking man with glasses and one of those Florida tans you can spot in a second in the jumble of pale-faced New York crowds in wintertime. He was smoking a pipe and it went well with his comfortable-looking office and his tweeds. He cleared his throat and smiled. He tilted back in his chair.

"You didn't tell me in your letter that you were Negro."

At least, I thought, he doesn't beat around the goddam bush. Aloud, I said, "I'm not required by law to tell you what I am."

"No," he said with a slow smile, "but perhaps we could do more for you under the circumstances if you had let us know."

I stared at him, waiting. I didn't know whether to admire him for his frankness or not.

"Your resumé," he said, looking down at it, "is excellent. The best one, as a matter of fact, we've got for this job. But I can't send you out."

"I wish," I said bitterly, "I could prove what you're saying."

He sat back and lighted his pipe. Suddenly he smiled. "Why?"

"You're liable for prosecution."

"That's one way," he said calmly. "But wouldn't it be better all around if you stopped butting your head against a stone wall? That's what you're doing now, you know. You look like a bright young fellow. Why don't you start a business with another Negro or even a group of you? That way you don't come in contact with this sort of nonsense. You could be successful."

"Mr. Graff, I don't believe that. I know from experience that it doesn't work." I was surprised that I could be so calm about something that mattered so much. "You said my resumé was the best you have for the job. I'm a little older, I guess, than most of the applicants—older because I've had to spend the time getting the experience that five years ago people like you used as an excuse for not giving me a job I was qualified for. Now there's no excuse. You simply tell me you can't send me out because I'm Negro.

"My best friend," I went on, and I was beginning to get angry, "is starving right now because he can't get a decent job, and he's got my experience beat ten times over and—"

"Hold on, Steve."

But I didn't. This comfortable-looking man, this kindly looking man, this intelligent and in some ways admirable man was telling me to go to hell because I was black.

"Maybe," I said, my voice rising. "Hitler had the right idea, after all!"

Then I stopped, but the words kept ringing in my ears and I wished I could shake them out because I hadn't wanted to say that, but it had come, surging over the barriers I had thought were very firm.

He looked at me, not unkindly, and there was an expression of infinite patience on his face and, more than that, understanding. I looked down at the floor and wanted it to open up and grab me. As badly as I felt about it, I didn't apologize. What the hell could an apology do to make up for *that*?

He sort of smiled and opened a desk drawer. He motioned me near him. "I want to show you something." He brought out some cards and placed them on the desk. "Look at these cards," he said. "They're from the dead files of an employment agency I worked for years ago. Doesn't matter how long ago—they haven't changed their practices at all."

He took out a pencil and pointed to a space on the cards in

133

which the interviewer's remarks were scribbled in ink. *Excellent* was the comment on the first card.

"You know what that means, Steve?"

"No."

"It's code. It means *Jewish, don't send out.*"

"Oh."

He picked up another card and pointed to another comment. "That means *Negro, don't send out.*"

"Do most agencies use codes to get around the law?"

"Most," he said, shuffling the cards back together. "A lot simply file the applications away and forget them. There are codes for Puerto Ricans, Catholics, Orientals and so on."

"Who else is there to discriminate against?"

He laughed. "You'd be surprised."

"But why don't you do something, if you're really concerned?"

"Oh, I don't know." He'd put the cards away and was now puffing on his pipe. He stared at the wall. "I'm married. I have a family, two kids in college. I have to make a living. Besides, I'm only one man. This work is my life and I would not know how to do anything else. You ask me to sacrifice reality for principle." He shook his head. "I can't do it alone. If all the other silent voices joined me, it might be a different story. No, I can't do it though I probably won't sleep well for the rest of the week because of you."

"But are you really living, Mr. Graff?"

He smiled again, that sudden smile. "You saw the office when you came through?"

I nodded and couldn't help smiling. It was some office.

"I have a home, a maid"—he chuckled—"no, she's not colored. She's German . . . and two cars. I'm living, Steve, such as it is."

"Well," I said, as he stood up, "thanks for the time." I started for the door.

"Steve," he called. I returned to his desk. He was frowning at my resumé. "I'm going to do something for you. I'm going to try to land you a job."

"Let me correct you, Mr. Graff."

134

He looked up; he was mildly surprised.

"You're going to do something for yourself if you land me a job."

The sudden smile again. "You're right, I guess. Something for myself. Now, it's going to be tough. I don't have to tell you. And it may not always be something in your line—"

"Mr. Graff, I have to stick to my line." I smiled as I said it. "I wouldn't know how to do anything else."

He slapped his leg and laughed until his pipe almost fell from his mouth.

"Besides," I said, more soberly, "I've got to."

"All right, Steve. That's fair enough—just as long as you understand that it's going to be tough."

"I understand."

"Your phone number's correct?"

"Yes. You'll call me? I shouldn't call you?"

"Call whenever you please, Steve."

We shook hands at the door.

"I'm sorry about that," I said. "What I said."

"Forget it, son." He looked at me appraisingly, then said, "I've had my moments when I thought Bilbo had been doing a fine job."

So we understood one another. Looking at him, I saw for the first time that his eyes were blue. Then, almost inexplicably, we laughed so loud that the receptionist smiled up at us.

"Now," he said, "my conscience gets up off its tail. That's why I've saved the cards."

I returned to the office feeling better than I had in weeks. It was a perfect time—as rain, slow and cruel, swept through the city— for Grace to call and say she'd be down the next day.

CHAPTER EIGHTEEN

I PLEADED ill at the office and took a couple of days off. I think Rollie was glad, because whenever I had the chance I usually gave him that I-have-something-on-you look. It seemed to bother him so I got kicks out of it.

I met Grace at the train. She didn't look like the mother of two Dennis-the-Menace-type boys. She came through the crowd smiling. She looked lovely, and walking out of that predominantly white crowd, she looked more attractive than ever. I took her bag and we walked north a half block on Vanderbilt. That way we were out of the crush of people waiting for cabs in the station driveway. We got one right away, before it turned into the station. We held hands in silence for a while, pausing only to look at one another and smile. Occasionally she would say something in a low voice, moving her lovely lips carefully and precisely so I would know what she was saying; she didn't want the cabbie to hear her.

We settled back. Traffic had gotten clogged up in the light rain.

"Were you surprised," she asked, "when I called?"

"Yes. How are the kids? Who's with them?"

"They're fine. They sent you these." She opened her purse and took out some drawings that had been folded. Nothing unusual; kid stuff.

I said, "They're fine. I'll have to write and thank them."

She laughed. "Mrs. Moody is with them. She's very nice and they love her." She sighed and threw herself back against the seat. "It's good to be back in New York. I want to relax a couple of days." She batted her lashes at me a couple of times, meaningfully. I chuckled and tweaked her on the knee.

"How come the time off?" I asked.

"Another strike. They're always having them. This one started at the Syracuse plant and spread."

"I was coming up Christmas," I said.

"So come up. We're planning on it."

"We?"

"All right. I."

"I hope you'll have a good time this week end."

She sat up. "What do you mean?"

I patted her hand. "Nothing, baby."

Still looking at me, she leaned back against the seat. "Once everything is in the open, it'll be all right. You'll see."

"Now what do *you* mean?"

She must have been feeling very good because she laughed again. "You've always been in love with me just as I've always been in love with you, Steve."

"So what?"

"So you might have done a little better than you did."

"It wouldn't have made any difference—you'd have walked out anyway. I have a feeling that even if I were in social work you wouldn't be happy, Grace. Anyway, Grant had what you thought you wanted—security."

"I waited a long time, Steve, and you know it. I think you were glad Grant was there. At least, then, he was between you and me, and you didn't have me nagging you for security."

"I wasn't in love with you anymore," I lied.

"And now?"

"Let's talk later," I said, indicating the cab driver. "Go through the park!" I told him.

"Aw right awready, buddy," he said. "I'm not in love wit' you."

We rode the rest of the way in silence. The cabbie shook his head when we got out. Grace didn't look at all contrite. Kittenish, rather, was the way she was, and I found I couldn't stay angry with her.

"I have to go to the store," I said when we'd got upstairs. I was out of liquor. "All you have to do is cook."

"All right."

She began whipping out of and into things. I slammed the door when I went out. All the way to the liquor store I thought of the jumbled relationships. My brother's wife; and my nephews would be my stepsons! Oh, hell.

"Yessir," the clerk said.

"Incest."

"What?"

I came to and told him what I wanted. He put the bottle in a bag and I returned home. Dinner was ready and I fixed drinks.

"Are you in love with me now?" She asked it leaning over my shoulder, her hair brushing against my cheek. In her hands was a plate filled with hot food, the like of which you couldn't buy anywhere in the city.

"Yes, I love you."

When I had cleaned my plate two or three times and sat back exhausted, she said, "You're a liar."

"Well, you do cook like hell. I love you for that."

"And that's all?"

"Oh, for Christ's sake, Grace. I love you. I love you, I love you." I stood up. "But then I don't love you."

"Going to be a little boy with me?"

"Whatever you say." I stalked to the bottle. "I wonder," I said, "if marrying you on your terms wouldn't be as big a defeat as my allowing these people to make me quit wanting what I mean to have."

"A defeat?"

"Yes."

"Everything's a battle, isn't it, Steve? You either win or lose."

"It isn't anything else, Grace. Hadn't you ever thought of it like that?"

"No, I hadn't. It seems to me that's not quite right."

"Maybe. But that's the way it is."

"You make it like that, Steve?"

"No, baby, I didn't."

"Then why?"

"Because it just is."

She traced her long fingers across her brow. "I don't understand.

What is it you want out of life? You've told me before. Tell me again."

"A little money, Grace. Enough so I don't have to sit around a couple of days waiting for Friday to roll around. Enough so I can go bury someone if it had to be done all of a sudden. And I'd like to have a house somewhere. I don't think I'd live in it all the time—I'd just like to have it. Most of all, I'd like to see the end of the day come knowing I'd done something worthwhile and not merely existed for that twenty-four hours. Grace, these are little dreams, and I don't really want much more—"

"Suppose, Steve, your dreams don't come true?"

I looked dumbly at the pitying smile playing on the edges of her mouth. I had never thought my dreams would not come true. It would take a long time, maybe, and perhaps there would be moments when the visions would be obscured completely, but they'd come true. I looked at Grace and had to drop my eyes.

"If they don't come true, then I just don't know."

"That's a little like the people who write books for your company, isn't it?"

"Yes, dammit!"

She turned away as though I'd hit her, and, again, silence came between us.

"Grace," I said earnestly, "you've got to have dreams. Haven't you ever had them?"

"I'm afraid to have them."

"Then why are you here?"

She didn't answer.

"Why are you here?"

"Because," she almost sobbed, "I *want* to have them, but I'm afraid to."

Almost, I thought, like Lois. Grace moved then; she had been sitting at the table, but now she got up and moved slowly, almost sadly about, removing dishes, placing them in the sink. She washed them and dried them and in all that time neither us said anything. But we did look at one another and we did try to smile. When she was finished, she sat down beside me.

"I want to say something."

"Say it, dear."

"I don't want you to get angry."

"Oh." I paused. "Well, say it anyway." I tried to pull her to me.

"No, don't. Wait until I finish. All right?"

"All right."

"Honey, you've got to realize that you are a Negro. You've got to live with it, settle down with it. I don't want you to feel that you have to fight, fight, fight." She looked at me. "Don't you ever give up?"

"Grace, you talk as if white folks raised you." I moved. "You want me to give up? Give up what, for God's sake? I'm scrambling and scuffling for the littlest things every hour of the day—the right to walk the streets in peace, the right to claim a job I can handle, the right to live where I choose because I like it and can afford it."

She tried to place her hands over her ears, but I took them away and held them.

"Ten years from now, baby, Frankie and Teddy may be out here dragging around trying to find jobs they're qualified for but can't get. Why? Because they're black—and, baby, they're not going to make any headway if I give up, if a hundred qualified niggers give up and call it quits. That's a part of the dream too, Grace."

"Don't shout," she said.

I didn't know I had been.

"Why are you so concerned with the boys?"

"Huh?" I said, to give myself a chance to think, to come back with an answer. Grace and her probing. "They're my nephews," I finally said. I lay back. I was tired and spent.

She said, "You're angry, Steve, and afraid."

"I am afraid—you're right. I wonder why it is that guys like me and Obie don't seem to fit. Ah, hell, be Negro." I sat up again. "Grace you've always known right from wrong, and to be willing to accept the rear seat offered to a Negro is as wrong as their pointing it out for you. Do you know what all this miserable fighting is about?"

140

"What? I'd like to know."

"In a sense it's sort of teaching them all over again the democracy they forgot or ignore."

"You're impossible." She turned, and I took her in my arms then and we didn't talk until minutes later when she said, "You think it's a defeat to marry me because I wouldn't let you fight and dream?"

"Yes. You wouldn't fight or dream with me."

"You love me?" This time she didn't ask to tease. She didn't sound confident, cocksure.

"For a long, long time. Maybe for always. Somehow it's a little different."

"You mean not as much?"

"No, just different."

"And if I wanted you to keep on fighting?"

"But you're not sure, baby—still, you'd be awful welcome to the team."

Women cry over the damnedest things. When she was over it, I touched the curves of her body, let my fingers rest lightly upon them, so that it could have been like touching the outline of a cloud. It had been a long time, she said. We kissed. Her mouth opened slowly and I pressed her down and soon I was moving beneath the arch of her arms.

The phone woke us the next morning. I went to answer it, and Grace, still kittenish, followed me. I kept thinking how alive and healthy her brown body looked. Once Lois had asked me if she looked sickening, her color, and I had said no, but I had not told her the truth. Sometimes, when I was with her, I could understand why suntanning was so popular.

And, damn, it was Lois on the phone.

"Are you feeling all right?" She rushed on before I could answer. "I had to talk to you and the urge became so great this morning that I called your office. They said you were out ill."

My mind was whirling. I hadn't seen or talked to Lois after that night in Yorkville. There had been times when I had wanted to call her.

"I'm fine," I said. "You?"

"You are ill, aren't you?" She sounded suddenly suspicious.

"Yes."

"Who's there? Man or woman? You're not sick." There was surprise, and a touch of humor, in her voice.

"Yes," I said.

Grace kissed me on the neck and made a loud noise—she suspected that I was talking to a woman. I mean, what can you do when they've got you in the middle?

"What's that noise?" Lois asked.

"I don't know."

"It is a woman, isn't it?" Her voice had become sad.

"Well . . ."

"Is it that woman from Albany?"

After a while I said, "Yes."

"Will you call me tomorrow?"

"Yes." Slowly I placed the receiver back upon its cradle.

Grace looked kind of foolish standing there nude with her hands on her hips. "One of your women?" she asked.

"Kid from the office."

"Oh."

She didn't say anymore. I suppose something in my expression told her I didn't want to talk about it. She didn't mention the call again.

When Grace and I went walking later, I half expected to see Lois lingering on the street somewhere, but I didn't and I was glad.

I enjoyed Grace's being there more then I thought I would. She had done very well what she had come for—to tell me it was all right, whatever I wanted to do. It was all very good, but I could not help wondering if Grant's ten thousand and her job security hadn't made the difference.

In the evening we shopped for the kids, then went downtown to sample coffees in the coffeehouses. On the way back uptown we stopped to visit Lint and Bobbie. We played darts with them. Grace got us out of an hour's game with a double one shot, confessing gleefully that she hadn't even aimed.

Later, at home, we lay talking quietly while Frank Sinatra did a bunch of things. We kept playing "Wee Small Hours" over and over again. That Sinatra. You can feel he enjoys singing. As Grace and I talked, my thoughts of Lois grew less and less frequent, then went away altogether.

Then it was morning. Grace was taking the Empire State out at seven-thirty. We woke, showered together and took a cab to the station. We checked her bag and got breakfast. A guy on the corner at Vanderbilt and 42nd was selling gardenias.

"How much?" I asked.

He looked at the bills, which I foolishly held in my hand, and said, "Two fifty."

Bastard, I thought, but it was too late—you let your guard down in this town and it's your butt. So I bought the gardenia and pinned it on Grace's coat. The vendor smiled as we walked away. Grace kept smiling down at the flower. We walked down the ramp again, into the smell of dust and oil and people. We followed the redcap to her seat. Grace kissed me good-bye and said, "Go on fighting, but please do something about me."

"Grant's money made the difference, didn't it?"

I couldn't hold it in any longer. Like a kid, I had to put her to the test. Always testing for truth and lie, fact and fantasy.

"I won't lie, Steve. It did."

"Before it was no and now it's come on."

"Yes. I can't lie about that either."

"Maybe I'll be up Christmas," I said.

I left her just as the conductors were beginning to shout their warnings. I waited beside her window until the train slid out, then I returned home. The place was empty, so empty. I thought of both Grace and Lois until my head hurt and I really didn't feel like going in to the office.

While I lay there on the bed trying to recall what Grace had felt like, the phone rang. It was Sarah, wanting to know if I felt well enough to come in because there was a lot of work. I told her I was still sick, and I was—sick of her. Her voice was filled with vague threats and I began to feel very uneasy, but I told her I just couldn't make it and that was that.

As I had promised, I called Lois, and because I was lonely and because I did want to see her, I talked her into having dinner with me. She agreed and I met her downtown. When she saw me, she broke into a smile and came running. We ate at a Chinese restaurant and while we were there, people watching us, she touched my wrist tenderly. I didn't try to hide from myself the fact that I enjoyed it, that inside I was gloating.

I had planned, some nights before, to spend the night looking for Obie and skip the party at Lint's he'd told Grace and me about. But now, with Lois' fingers soft on my skin, I had to admit it did something to me every time she'd run out of the lobby of her building to meet me; that I got a bang out of the way she skipped through heavy traffic to get to the other side of the street where I was. I liked the way she smiled suddenly if we met on the bus and I enjoyed the way she was when it was time for us to part. I decided to forget about Obie just then.

We started to get high. It was sort of a celebration, Lois said, what with not seeing each other for such a long time and with Christmas coming on. I got off to a flying start, perhaps because I hadn't really shaken the thought of parting. I was about half-stoned when I realized I had been doing a lot of drinking recently.

We finished dinner and walked through the Village. It was beginning to snow lightly. Lois showed me the place where she baked her ceramics. Passing through Washington Square she said, "What shall I get you for Christmas?"

"Scotch."

"No, you need gloves." She took one of my hands and rubbed it against her cheek.

"Cold," she said. "And I know it won't come off."

We cracked up laughing.

We saw a man sitting on a bench in the light snowfall. The way he sat, he might have been sunning himself in Miami.

"There he is," I said. "There can't be anyone quite that cool in the world."

We cracked up again. I mean, we were high.

"Oh!" she said, "I'm so high!" Her eyes were lustrous and very big in the dark. "Aren't you?"

"Yes, I'm high."

"You don't look it—you don't act it."

"I am high. Gloriously, magnificently." I kissed her and lifted her in the air. "See?"

She was satisfied. We took the bus uptown and because we were high we didn't care about the people who looked as we held hands. And we went to the party.

If Lint and Bobbie were surprised to see Lois after having seen Grace the night before, they didn't show it. Lint, seeing Lois for the first time, was taken with her resemblance to his wife. Bobbie was high. She took Lois and showed her around, laughingly introducing her as her sister because they looked so much alike. Lint and I went to the kitchen to get drinks and he said, "That Lois—" and he shook his fingers as if they'd touched something hot. "And Grace?"

Later, after I had shrugged off his question about Grace, he said, "You know, for an ugly guy, you do pretty well."

And he was damned glad of it, I bet, because that meant less time for me to spend "pursuing his wife."

We rejoined the mob of people there. Lois mixed easily, as she always did, not showing any signs of hesitation or awkwardness; she was perfectly composed. The party wolves were on the make for her—they could not conceive that she'd come with me—but she was always looking for me.

"Steve?"

"Here, baby."

"Dear, why don't you stay in one place?"

I laughed and placed an arm around her. The party grew wild. Lint and Bart got into a mock knife duel and Bart got cut on the wrist. Bobbie didn't like the way Lint was fondling women, so while he was sitting on the couch, she hurled a dart at him. It stuck in the cushion just outside his shirtsleeve. Lint didn't move. It was almost as though he expected or wished to get a dart in the heart.

145

Aiming another, Bobbie said, "You don't have to be so goddam obvious about it." The second dart also barely missed him.

"You want me to be like you, you sneaky bitch?" he asked, and just before Bobbie threw the third one I whirled her away in a Calypso. The party hadn't come to a halt at all—everyone was doing just what they'd been doing before. And this, I thought, was the middle-class society I wanted to belong to. This is it! Nothing.

"I want to go home," Lois said. "These people frighten me."

We went out then and sat on the stairs a few minutes, listening to a couple of homosexual actors argue. I cupped Lois' face in my hands and kissed her.

"We've got to stop!" she said, squeezing my hand. "I still wait for you to call and when you don't I get angry. And that woman yesterday . . ." she said, then stopped.

Finally we got up and started walking home, walking away from the party, the middle-class livers, the artists who knew it all, did it all and had all the inside poop on every damned thing.

"Come upstairs," I said as we paused by my place.

"No."

I didn't insist and I walked her down to her building. "Let me shop with you tomorrow," I said. She was going to pick up some things for Christmas.

"Will you?"

"Yes," I said.

After work the next afternoon I met her at Bloomingdale's, where I loped around behind her. For some reason she kept thinking she'd lost me and was always stopping to look for me. Once I remarked, "Well, let's get the kids' shopping done for Christmas," and people around us became startled and shot quick looks at us, first her, then me. Cool New York. Yeah!

Lois laughed and said, "Idiot."

When we finished shopping, we found a quiet bar on Third Avenue and had a drink.

"I don't think," she said, "we'd better see each other again."

"All right."

"We can't let it go any further."

"No."

"Don't be like that."

"Like what?"

"Like you are."

About an hour later we walked down the block where we lived. I stopped in front of my place. "Come on up, baby," I said.

"No."

"Baby . . ."

She started to come. She walked, head lowered, halfway up the steps. Then she whirled suddenly and rushed down again, saying breathlessly, "Oh, Steve!"

I watched her as she walked quickly toward her building and I knew she was terribly confused and flushed. I think I was smiling a little to myself as I went inside.

CHAPTER NINETEEN

I GUESS the season was upon me. Anyway, I decided to do something constructive and I spent a few frantic days searching for Obie, but I couldn't find him. I received, by mail, the gloves from Lois with a little note saying she was going to the Island so she wouldn't fall prey to the holidays and weaken. I smiled when I read that.

I've always loved Christmas. We always managed to have nice ones when we were young, even if the Christmas dinner was neckbones and rice with a few scrawny yams on the side. Christmas was the only time I consciously wished every man only the best of luck in his sorrowful little rat race.

Feeling this way, I couldn't help but make the trip to Albany. There was snow all the way up, soft, clean snow; white snow as yet untouched by dust and filth. Once on the train, I knew I was going to enjoy being with Grace and the kids. I hoped Lois, too, was having a good time.

There was ice on the river. Ducks swam gingerly between the gray floes and I noticed that there was not a single duck alone, bobbing on the current; there were always two. Always. And that made me think of Obie and Gloria, and I wished them a good time. I wished the best of the seasons also to Hadrian Crispus, who had threatened to come to New York and find out for himself what was going on. Rollie hadn't answered his letters and it got to the point that when a letter from him began to arrive every day, Sarah would laugh harshly and announce, "Another one from the farmer."

I forgot about all of them when Grace and the boys met me at the station. Frankie and Teddy were so thickly padded with clothes that they looked as though they'd bounce back up if they fell down, like rolypolies. We took a taxi home and it was like all the Christmases I remembered as a child—the big wreaths all over the windows, the tree weighted down with decorations, and underneath, presents. The house was filled with the odors of cooking—turkey, mince, onions, spices. I met Mrs. Moody, a widow who lived alone next door. She was helping Grace with the next day's dinner, and sharing Christmas with her and the boys. Mrs. Moody reminded me of my mother. Maybe it was because it was Christmas, or perhaps because I was a little high again.

That was why I took the kids out to bellywhop—I *was* high. While we were out there, Teddy, with that big, wise smile kids have, said, "Is our mother going to marry you, Uncle Steve?" He started to slide, then stopped and came back to me. "Can we call you just Steve then, without the 'uncle'?"

"Sure, I don't care. Hey, listen, Teddy."

"Huh?" He hoisted his sled impatiently.

"Let me slide."

"I want to slide first," he said. "Besides, you might break it."

He dashed off then, swinging his sled back and forth in that clumsy manner kids have, and slid down the slope to join his brother. Once he looked back at me as if to figure me out and, maybe because he was feeling sorry for not having let me slide, he smiled and tried to wave and fell off the sled. I wanted to run to him, but something made me stop. Teddy got up and brushed himself off and trudged back to the top of the hill, where I was standing. He didn't say anything. He started running again and, puffing with each little stride, he was down the hill again. This time he waved and stayed on the sled. I waved back to him. A good, gutty kid. I liked that.

Both of them were making it up the hill again, puffing. Sometimes when I was with them there were moments when I seemed not even seconds older than they; then we had a lot of fun. But there were also those moments when they suddenly became aware that I was an adult. I'd always liked kids. When they are without the cunning they sometimes learn so quickly for survival, their presence here really seems providential.

Teddy and Frankie were precocious. Frankie attended a special school for painting and Teddy was in an advanced class in the same school. In them, it seemed, all the generations of our family had put forward their best—from Grace's family and mine. Watching them bang down the slope again, it occurred to me that it was they who would finally gain the fulfillment I had sought in my life, as my father had in his and his father before him. They seemed equipped to accept that fulfillment, to take it in stride. I suddenly wanted with all my heart to be with them or be a part of them when that happened. I also knew, as they began potting me with snowballs, that I had to prepare, as best I could, the way for them. My father had done that for me; now I could do it for them only because he gave me the opportunity to derive more from life than he had himself.

Later, we watched all the Christmas shows on television. I held Frankie in my lap and it was wonderful to feel his little body, his lean little thighs which would soon grow strong and long, and his big head warm against me. I felt very good; it was as if I had been swimming alone in the middle of an ocean for a long time and had suddenly found land. I got the boys ready for bed. They insisted that we sing carols because the day after next, Christmas would be gone and you had to stop singing carols then until just before next Christmas.

"You bitch," I said to Grace when the house was all settled down for the night. She had given me a big, wonderful dose of what it would be like to be with her. She smiled like a master swordsman who has just wounded you, and with your dying breath you're complimenting him, gallantly, on his skill. She only smiled.

"Fix the couch for me, will you?" I said.

"No."

"Grace, please fix it."

"If I do, will you come in later?"

"No," I said. I had decided that earlier, when I was on the hill with the kids.

"Why not?"

"Damn it, you know why not."

"They'll be asleep."

"I don't care." I know too many people who are still a little twisted from discovering "uncles" in their mother's beds.

"Then I'll come to you."

"No, Grace. Listen, they might get up and then what? I wouldn't want that to happen, so, please, good night and don't stand there tormenting me. I really don't want to do anything foolish and neither do you."

"Sometimes," she said, "you can be so good you make me sick. Good night!"

The next day, Christmas, went quickly. There were more shows on television and good food; there was the playing with toys; and the bright day began to darken as Grace and I exchanged glances more and more often. But I didn't try to settle anything with her. I had to get the job thing licked first. I had to get something good, something I could and wanted to do.

Back in New York again, I got set for New Year's. Where, I wondered, had the year gone? Crispus' mail was coming in just as steadily as ever, but his letters were beginning to seem incoherent. I showed them to Rollie, who laughed them off. The holiday had been hectic for him too. His eyes were red all the time and he looked bushed. Once I couldn't resist asking him in a low voice if he'd been making out okay. As soon as I said it, I knew it was the wrong thing to say for a guy who wanted to keep his job a little longer. Rollie didn't answer. That period, I didn't bother him for my raise and he didn't bother me; we were a little like boxers, each waiting for an opening.

I was glad to see Obie again. He'd called the office and, over the phone, I talked him into going to a couple of parties with me. He looked very haggard when he showed up. His first words were curt: "Nothing, nothing, nothing."

He hadn't found anything.

But we talked and drank and got a slight glow on. We were going to forget the hard times—his and the ones I saw coming for me. We went shopping for a good-luck dinner—black-eyed peas and pig's feet. We cooked the stuff, more or less, and began drinking again.

Later we went to a party in the Village where everyone was talking art and the handling of problems. Someone had dug up an old Tampa Red side, "It's Tight Like That," and we played it until we couldn't get anything but scratches from it. There were Bessie Smith blues too. When everyone got high, the party was good. Obie, standing a little aside, as though he felt he had no right to be there with his problems, said to me, "They all seem so—*happy*."

I looked at him. I didn't know what to say. I went back to the drinks. I didn't want to think of Grace and the kids, or of Lois or Rollie or the future. I just wanted to get a headful. And yes, dammit, I wanted to forget about Obie a little, too, because I wanted to be happy for a bit and Obie was too much a part of me for happiness to come if I thought about him. Lights began to hurt my eyes. Nothing seemed important except having a feverishly good time. I danced without a letup; something in me wanted to keep moving, moving, all the time moving. Once I saw Obie standing thin and austere beneath a light as the dancers parted for an instant, and I grew angry with him.

When we left the place to make the uptown party, I didn't have too much to say to him. On the way up, the horns, chimes and sirens sounded.

"Happy New Year," I said to Obie and the cabbie.

"Happy New Year, fellas," the cabbie said.

"Yeah," Obie grunted.

The second apartment was also filled with noise and people, but here they were all one color—colored. Big Joe Williams sang loudly. There was more music, women, dancing. Swift, darting repartee. Food. And still more music. There were suddenly harsh lights, people in bedrooms, paper cups filled with drinks, other drinks spilled. A quick red glow of a cigarette in a darkened bathroom and the smell of potiguaya. Smile, goddamit, Obie—just one smile, man!

Cha-cha-cha, sensuous, arrogant, elbow-moving, belly-moving, ass-moving. Do it, baby! One more time and after that, one more again.

"I love you, baby, I've always loved you. What's your name?"

"That's pretty. It's lovely. What is it again?"

"Your what? Why the hell didn't you tell me?"

Every day I have the blues . . .

"Aw, sing it, Joe!"

"Big Joe, Big Joe, do it, my man!"

"Baby, I can sing."

"Then sing, sugar."

". . . pussy that won't quit."

"I don't believe you."

"You'll never find out, sugar. Aw, sing it, Big Joe, sing it!"

And somewhere Bird began playing and somebody said, "Stop breathing, bitch, so I can hear the record."

A whirligig.

I resolved not to drink so much after New Year's; I drank at least five toasts to that. When dawn came slanting through Central Park, the party was still going and Obie was still in his corner, his clothes loose upon him and his face long and dry. I left him. I don't know how I got home, but I remember walking in from the street and saying to the chill air, "Hello, New Year. Please, baby, be good to me, please."

Sometime in the next few hours I woke up to go to the bathroom.

The walls were covered with roaches. I reached up and dragged my hand through the midst of them, expecting to see a clean swath when my hand came away. Nothing happened. The roaches were still there, twisting and squirming, their ugly backs brown and bright. I raised my hand to the wall and again nothing happened. I blinked my eyes and the roaches were gone. I returned to bed shaking and terribly cold.

The holidays were over.

That same week, determined to begin the New Year right, I went looking for another apartment. If I found one that was not too expensive, but had room enough, I'd make Obie move in with me for a while.

There was a routine I used when looking for an apartment. I didn't wear slacks and sport jacket but a suit, and shined my shoes. If you wear a suit and tie, people sometimes hesitate before refusing you; you could be anyone from anyplace, even if you were Negro. But they could refuse you, as the landlord of a place around the corner did.

At another place I threatened to take the landlord's name, and when I did, he let me see the apartment off Central Park West, which was no improvement over mine. I was refused at still another place and I took down the building code number and reported it to the State Commission Against Discrimination, which had moved into some phases of housing.

A week later, in response to their letter, I was in the SCAD office; they were unable to touch the landlord because he hadn't used either state or federal funds for his building.

"But let us know any time you run into this," I was told.

"I'd be writing or calling every day," I said.

"We're doing the best we can," the man said.

"Thanks," I said, and going out I thought, the best is never good enough anymore; it hasn't been for a long, long time.

So the New Year got off to a bad start. Obie came around again, a much different Obie Robertson from the one I had met the summer before. His mustache was ragged; he didn't seem to care about his clothes fitting or matching up. There were long silences in our conversations. After three quarts of beer, he opened up quietly.

"Steve, I'm a little afraid."

The words walloped across my stomach. All of us have fear; we spend the better part of our lives secreting it away. When someone says he has fear he's plugging into his listener. But mine wasn't as big as Obie's. As precarious as my position was, I preferred it immensely to his. He reminded me of a combat GI on the verge of becoming battle-hardened or nose-diving into a Section Eight.

"I can't believe," he said, "that this thing is so massive without form, and so rigid without apparent strength." He chopped his hands in the air, forming an imaginary square. "There's got to be a flaw in me." He thrust himself in the chest with a stiff forefinger. "It can't be the thing, it's got to be me."

It might have been me talking, I thought, as Obie's tired voice droned on. If he'd been with me a year ago in L.A., I would have said the same things to him. Instead, I told them to my brother. But now it wasn't me, it was Obie. I felt, watching him, the hopelessness my brother Dave must have sometimes felt watching me.

"What if your flaw isn't big enough to warrant all this?"

I might have hit him across the back with a bat, the way he winced.

"Then it's got to be the other thing, the discrimination, Steve. But I"—I couldn't stand the way his eyes pleaded, not Obie Robertson's eyes—"can't believe discrimination can be *this* horrible." He shook his head. "No, I can't believe it. I've got a flaw and I've got to work it out. I've been trying to, but—"

What would America be without people like Obie who say I am to blame, not you? I felt wild and reckless and I moved quickly and foolishly because my eyes had begun to smart. I broke into loud, stupid song:

> You got a flaw,
> I got a flaw,
> All god's chillun got flaws.
> When you get to heav—

154

Obie started up suddenly and ran out. I dashed into the hall shouting, "Obie! Obie! I'm sorry!" He didn't stop. "Stay in touch!" He didn't answer.

CHAPTER TWENTY

THERE were young men coming into the office with portfolios nearly every day now, and I could hardly work for thinking that Rollie was interviewing people to take my place. And I hadn't turned up anything yet. Between the job situation and Obie, I was sleeping little, and had become surly and quiet. I spent my evenings trying to do something constructive but doing very little of that.

About that time, my phone began ringing late at night. When I picked it up and said, "Hello," there was no answer, just a click at the other end. One night as I was walking past it, it rang and I snatched it up. "Hello," I barked. There was a sharp intake of breath at the other end. I could sense confusion.

"Hello," Lois said. Her voice was sheepish.

"How are you?"

"All right. I didn't expect you to be home." There was a pause. "I wanted to talk to you, but I didn't want you to be home."

"Doesn't make sense."

"You understand."

"Haven't seen you around," I said.

"I use the subway mostly now."

"Oh."

"How's the work?"

"Lousy."

"Are you getting things done at home?" She meant the free-lance writing.

"Not much."

"Haven't you been able to turn up anything jobwise?"

"Nothing, honey."

"Oh, gee." She sounded like a little girl.

"How are you making it with the head-shrinker?"

"We talk a lot about you."

"You do?"

"Well, I tell him how much I still—still love you."

"But why?"

"I tell him how good you are for me," she said. "He doesn't agree, of course."

"Course not."

"I told him we had stopped seeing each other," she rushed on, "but tonight, I felt I had worked at it so hard that I deserved something special, something good, like talking to you, even if you were home."

"Well . . . I'm glad you called—and that I was home."

"So am I—now. How was your holiday?"

"Pretty good. And yours?"

"Deadly."

Then she began talking about her parents and how if it were not for them, things could have been so different with us.

"Stop it." I paused. "Will you have some coffee, baby?" I guess maybe I shouldn't have tossed that question at her. It was sort of a curve, I realized.

"Again, I don't know what to say. I only wanted to talk to you."

"Wasn't there more to it than that?"

"No, dear, I swear it."

"How about the coffee?"

"You know we shouldn't, Steve."

"Yet you called me," I reminded her.

"I wish I hadn't now. Everytime I do, I seem to lose hold of everything. I want to see you, but—"

"All right. Forget it."

Her voice came very small then. "Just coffee?"

"Just coffee."

She came and we had coffee. "You look the same," she said. "Better, even."

"You look wonderful," I said. I avoided touching her and when she wrapped her arms around my back I didn't respond.

"You are being good, aren't you?"

I shrugged. When we finished the coffee I took her home.

"You have a date or something?"

"No, you wanted coffee. That's what I invited you here for. We've had it and I've brought you home."

She stood facing me, her back against a wall in her lobby. She turned and placed her forehead against it. "I know, I know."

"See you tomorrow?" I asked.

She nodded; she seemed very tired. "Yes, dear."

I left. I didn't feel good about what I'd done. The generations of phony taboos should have steered me clear of Lois, just as the ones she'd learned should have kept her from knowing me. I don't know why or where they broke down. I know only that she came spinning out of the blackness of time from one side of the world, and I from another, like two meteors birthed in opposite ends of the universe, rushing along in nothingness until they collide because they were destined to in the scheme of things.

It was true that she'd made the first overtures, but it was also true I had wanted her to make them, and perhaps this was why she did. If she hadn't, we wouldn't have been as we were a few days after the last coffee incident lying arm in arm in the darkness smoking.

She had come about an hour before. She said she thought she had seen Lint on the way over. We were pretty quiet in general; we hadn't had much to say to each other in the hour she'd been here.

"What are you thinking?" I asked her.

"Europe. Some parts of it with you." She laughed softly and buried her mouth in my neck.

"Funny, not to ever think of America," I said.

"I had thought about it, but each time I think of Yorkville, the idea becomes very sad."

"It's nice here like this," I said. I put my arm around her.

"That's because of you."

"Is it now?"

"Yes."

"I think it's because of you."

"I said it first," she said.

She was staring into space. I studied her unnoticed; her hair, the back of her neck, the slope of her shoulders. Even her ears. Lois turned suddenly and caught me looking. She gave me a soft, wondering smile. "What is it, dear?"

I felt suddenly as I had that night with Rollie. I wanted to tease Lois into showing her colors, white or black. "Lois?"

"Yes, Steve. What's the matter?"

"Let's get married."

She sat straight up and she tried to say everything at once, but what came out was: "No! I couldn't! Not ever!" And she shook her head vigorously. Then I sat up. I hadn't expected so violent a rejection. She touched my hand. "I—I didn't—" She shook her head and tried to smile. "Your question took me by surprise, dear."

I removed my hand. I got up and started walking around, all around the room. And then around some more. I had got my answer—why the hell was I walking?

"Then it was and is true, isn't it, Lois?"

"What, Steve?" She looked frightened.

"You used me as a tool against your parents—against your mother. You wanted to get even with her, Lois."

"No, no, no."

"For Christ's sake, stop and think. Your mother gave you a hard time, Lois. She still does—but, boy, if she knew you were sleeping with a Negro, wouldn't she be fit to be tied? Wouldn't she, Lois? Aren't you happier knowing if she knew it she would drop dead in her tracks?"

"No," she said, but she didn't say it convincingly.

"I knew it the very first night we slept together," I said. Her eyes widened. "But I sat on it." I was still walking and talking, like a goddam fool. "I didn't do anything, I didn't say anything, and do you know why, Lois?"

She was up now and she squeezed her fists to make her body stop shaking. "Because I used you too, baby. Oh, hell, I'm not clean in this. You had many faces, Lois, and I realize now I hated every white one of them. Nearly every time I called you, it had been a bad day for me, and I had to get back, if not at them directly, at you, and that worked out fine. It kept me from going nuts."

"I don't believe you."

"What is it you can't accept, Lois—that Negroes can think and feel and want revenge? Is that what your lily-white mind tells you?"

"I don't believe you, I don't."

"Then why are you shaking? Why don't you stop trembling?"

"I can't help it."

"You wanted revenge for the way your folks treated you. I wanted revenge for the way people treated me. We're even. Retaliation all around." I paused and took a deep breath. "I guess that's it, Lois. I don't think there's much sense stretching this out then, is there? I suppose you may as well go now."

She took a step toward me. "Can't we talk about—"

I had already started shaking my head. What the hell was there to talk about?

There was a pounding on the door; it shivered along its hinges.

"Let me in, Steve." It was Lint. He was shouting. "Damn it, I saw Bobbie come in here. I caught you this time, didn't I, you bastard. Open this goddam door before I break it in!"

He rushed against it. *Bam*!

"Lint," I said. "Bobbie's not here. This is someone else." I looked around at Lois, wondering if I should tell Lint she was here, not his wife, but I didn't recall Lint ever being so angry and I couldn't be sure he wouldn't track Lois down and call her a liar for standing up for me and hurt her. Lois had been hurt enough. "Lint, will you listen to me? Bobie's not here! This is *not* Bobbie, man."

"You black sonovabitch, I'll kill you, Steve. So help me, I'll kill you."

"You're drunk, Lint."

"I'm going, Steve, but I'll be back, God damn you, and I'll kill you."

I heard him stomp down the hall. I sat down and lighted a cigarette. Lois slumped down in a chair, sniffled, then fumbled out a cigarette of her own. We sat that way, smoking, not speaking, for about fifteen minutes. Then I said, "I guess it should be all clear now."

"Thanks for not involving me."

"I was thinking of Lint."

"Thanks anyway."

"Good-bye, Lois."

"Good-bye, Steve."

I held the door open for her. She started through it, then stopped. "What can I say?"

I said, "You've said it."

She looked thoughtful and walked off. I watched her go down the hall and turn out of sight. I closed the door and locked it. I went to bed wondering where Bobbie was. I wondered if she'd return to Lint that night, or was this it, the time she'd picked for leaving him?

I was feeling out of sorts the next morning and it had to be the day Hadrian Crispus came to the office.

He came in just before noon. Rollie had arrived about a half hour before. Crispus walked through the door without saying anything, passing Leah who watched him enter Rollie's office. She rushed in to call me.

"Crispus is here and he doesn't look right."

"Who?"

"Crispus, Crispus. *O, Come Ye Back*."

"Shhh!" I said.

The voices—Crispus' and Rollie's—were coming loud and sharp from Rollie's office. They built up to a crescendo, followed by a silence. There was a sudden gagging noise.

"Go see! Go see!" Leah urged me, just as Sarah and Anne came rushing in from the john.

"It's Crispus!" Sarah said. "He's mad! Mad!"

I went in thinking of Crispus' letters, the sound of them; the way they were scrawled and the way Rollie ignored them. When I caught sight of the man, Crispus had Rollie by the neck and was squeezing very slowly.

"Crispus," I said, but he didn't bother to turn. Rollie saw me behind Crispus and his eyes went big with pleading. "Crispus!" I said again, more sharply this time. Still he didn't turn.

I picked up a chair, poised it for an instant over his head, then brought it down. It shattered into bits, little whole bits. I looked stupidly at them as Crispus sank to the floor.

Sarah hustled to a phone and in minutes the police were there, and Crispus, his head bleeding, was taken away. Sarah walked in and out with cold cloths for Rollie, saying "He's mad, that man. Absolutely mad, I tell you. Look what he did."

Late in the afternoon Rollie came in to thank me.

"Forget it," I said, not wanting to talk about it.

I left the office early, hating every atom of the place. I knew I'd have my job a little longer, thanks to Hadrian Crispus, but I didn't know how much longer I could take it. The events of the past evening had left me tired and discouraged.

I let my feelings about Crispus and Rollie juggle around on the bus home. What were my feelings really? I couldn't say for sure what I'd wanted to happen. Let Crispus kill Rollie? I had been a little slow getting there. Let them kill each other? Why not? I hated Rollie for his astute and horrible juggling of economics and sociology in taking advantage of me. And I disliked Crispus for his prejudice. I didn't know which was worse.

When I got home I thought of Lois. I wondered when, if ever, she would realize that what she thought was love stemmed from revenge. I hoped she would, and I hoped she'd work things out with her doctor. After all, he was getting twenty bucks a session. It was with a vague feeling of relief that I turned to thinking of Grace, Teddy and Frankie, and later on in the evening it became a damned good feeling, thinking about them. Still later, Obie called and I invited him to lunch the next day, feeling even better because Lint had not come.

CHAPTER TWENTY-ONE

THERE was not much doing in the office in the morning, so I left for lunch early to meet Obie. He was late and I ordered without him. I was halfway through my meal when I glanced at the door again and saw Obie entering, shambling between the tables toward me. I got an odd feeling the moment I saw him.

"Jesus," I said to myself. Obie looked so damned lean. And he seemed insensitive to everything; he just kept shambling. I hoped people wouldn't notice him the way I did. He bumped into tables and waiters and didn't turn around. He just kept coming ahead as if he'd been wound up and would keep moving until the machinery stopped.

"Hey, man," he greeted me. He sounded very tired. He was trying to be his old flip self. He tried to smile, but it was a queer smile that hung on his wretched face.

"Sit down, man," I said.

Obie tried to grin. He looked at the food on my plate. "I'm a little late. Forgive me, man."

"It's all right." I could not rid myself of that feeling of uneasiness. "Order."

The waitress came and Obie slowly gave her his order.

"Nothing?" I asked, meaning the job situation.

"No," he answered briefly.

He slumped back in his chair and watched the diners.

"Once," he said, "when things were real bad, man, I mean bad, I took a job nights as a clean-up man in a bank. I had to tall all sorts of damned lies to get the job. They destroyed money in the bank. Pieces of it stuck to my shoes every night and I couldn't get it off. I know I couldn't have pieced it together, but anyway, I like to have flipped with so many pieces of money underfoot," he finished softly.

"Allegory?"

He merely sighed. The waitress came with his plate.

162

"I was thinking about going back to a job like that for a while," he said, "if I could lie my way into it." He looked up and tried to smile again. "Man, I got so good on that job, I could go to sleep standing up, holding the broom in my hands. The minute I heard the elevator doors open, I automatically stepped forward, pushing the broom. By the third step I was wide awake and the boss never caught on."

He gave a weird laugh. He reached for things on his plate and put them back. He made me nervous. "It gets harder and harder to go back like that. It's almost as though they won't *let* you go back and won't let you get forward." He looked archly at me. "Even if you did want to compromise."

Obie talked without looking at me. I might just as well not have been there. Only once had he looked directly at me. It was as if he was trying to hide something. I had another cup of coffee. Obie tried to eat from habit. He kept looking up from his plate with the oddest, hangdog appearance, still without looking at me. Then he placed his fork carefully alongside his plate.

"Steve, I'm *tired*, awfully *tired*. Not afraid anymore—just *tired*."

He leaned toward me and still managed not to look at me. The way he had said *"tired"* jarred me. "You know something? That flaw we talked about . . ."

Hypnotized, I nodded.

"It's not the flaw—"

"Obie," I said, "Obie," and I had a fleeting image of my brother Dave sitting beside me, helpless. "Listen, Obie, things gotta break." I wanted the words to have weight and power and strength in them. I wanted them to knock him down and make him get up fighting and angry. "This afternoon," I said desperately, "you're moving in with me. I've had enough of you and your goddam pride. So let's go get your stuff, man."

I stood up, but Obie remained at the table, smiling for the first time. I sat down again. "Obie, you can't go nowhere but up, man, and you know I'm with you all the way. Obie, I *got* to be with you, you know that. You know you're my nigger, man."

He smiled again and dropped his head. "Knock it off, man."

"Look," I said when we finally got outside. "I'll take the afternoon off and pop to a show. What do you say?"

His face had become set again. "Naw, I got a couple of things to do."

"Tonight then," I insisted.

"Date tonight," he mumbled.

"Obie—"

"Leave me alone, for Christ's sake!" he snarled at me, shaking off my arm. Then in a more normal tone he said, "I'll be talking to you, man. Cool it."

He shuffled toward Fifth Avenue, bustling and jammed with people on the move. Riveting and clanging sounded from the magnificent new structures going up; the construction workers swarmed arrogantly and sure-footed along the steel beams and girders. Cabbies yelled, cops blew whistles. So many people, it seemed, and every damned one of them had something to do or someplace to go.

That night I tried not to drink so much, and I managed pretty well. I was only a little high when I heard running down the hall and pounding at the door. I knew it was Lint.

"Open the door, you sonovabitch!" he shouted. "I'm gonna kill you!"

I heard him back off and then he slammed against the door. I heard him back off again and I unlocked the door and pulled it open as he rushed forward, past the open door clear to the other side of the room. I ignored him, turned my back to him and closed the door. I thought it would help cool him off.

It didn't.

When I turned, he was there, grasping for my throat. He practically lifted me off the floor. I grabbed his wrists and hung on. He'd been drinking, but he wasn't drunk. He had two days growth of beard and his eyes were red-rimmed and wild. I imagined he'd been running all over town trying to find Bobbie. She hadn't returned then. His shouts banged and crashed into my ears. He clobbered me and lights began flashing all over the place, and I found myself trying to talk to him.

"Lint, Jesus, wait a minute, will you? That wasn't Bobbie here the other night, that was Lois. You said yourself they looked alike—"

Splat! The floor came up to meet me.

"I'da been here last night, black boy, only I didn't figure you'd have the nerve to hang around with my wife here. I been running to the stations and the airports. Even up in Harlem, where you belong, nigger. You hear me, *nigger*? N-I-G-G-E-R!" He rushed at me again and I slipped, spun away from him. "What does she like, Sambo—your great big black dick? Is that it? You got one, I know. *All* niggers got 'em."

He reached in his pocket and slipped out the knife he'd used in his mock duel with Bart at the party. "I'm goin' to get rid of that weight for you, nigger. I'm going to cut it off. But she's going to see this, too. She's going to know what I'm doing to you. Where the hell is she?"

"Under the bed," I said.

He dropped to the floor and peered under the bed. "Come out of there, you bitch. I'm going to give you a present!"

He waved his arm beneath the bed. Then he realized I had duped him. He turned and looked up at me quickly, and fright, for the first time, showed on his face. He looked at my hands. I lifted them and showed there was nothing in either of them.

"Get up," I said.

If this was to be it, well, what the hell, it was just it, and I felt myself begin to tremble, the way I always did when the anger and fear collided. He looked at me and I could see his senses starting to come back.

"Lint," I said, and I wished I could make my voice stop shaking. I was so damned tense. I was going to kill me a white man within the next few minutes. I quivered from head to foot like a taut piano wire. "Get on your goddam feet."

His eyes flashed to the knife in his hand.

"Keep it or throw it away," I said. "It doesn't make any difference."

He tossed it away and I saw in his eyes something wild and savage.

He moved slowly, gathering his legs beneath him. I stepped back to give us room. For some reason Obie's racked face flashed before me. I was almost crying now, the urge to get my hands on Lint and kill was so strong.

"Get up, you bastard! C'mon, get up!"

So it had all come down to this, then. All that I was and all that had happened to me—was it all to explode here in one wild minute in my room? All the way down to this—Lint Mason here in his crazy mind to castrate me and show his wife?

"Lint?"

He was up now, his eyes quick and feverish and some of the madness back in them. His shoulder moved up to protect his chin. His fists climbed upward.

"I've swallowed your crap a long time, Lint, not because you're white, as you seem to think now, but because I thought we were friends and, God, how I had need of friends."

"You black sonovabitch!" he screamed. "Fight!"

Even then I could admire him for not coming apart at the seams before what he knew had to come. Unless maybe he wanted it to come.

Anyway, I moved.

I double-feinted, dropping my right shoulder, then my left. Then I drove in above his shoulder with my right, felt my knuckles dig cleanly into his jaw. His head bounced away. He swung back blindly, carrying his weight low and flashing the now unconcealed hatred in his eyes at me. He caught me just above the eye and I went down, near the knife. I didn't want it. I wanted him with my hands and I almost laughed when he kicked it away, like in the movies.

He caught me then, as I came up and bounced me off the wall. I came back and put both hands into that belly that had grown fat, the way I'd seen Sugar Ray do it—three, six, eight times, so fast you couldn't count them. He humped his stomach in, bringing his chin down, and I reached way back and steamed in with the right, again and again and again. He went down, then started back up, but I put a foot beside his head and bounced him back to the floor.

"Nigger!" he spat.

I kicked him again. His head was bleeding, and his nose, too. I was cut up some, myself. There was blood above my eye and a salty taste in my mouth; a tooth was gone. Maybe I'd swallowed it. I stradled Lint and hooked rights and lefts into his face. He brought his arms up to cover his face, but I held them down with one hand and hit him with the other. Each time I hit him he called:

"Nigger!"

And I kept swinging. "You're gonna die, white man," I panted.

"Nigger!"

Splat!

"Nigger!"

"You're gonna die, Lint. You know that?"

"Nigger!"

Splat! Splat!

Then I couldn't hit him anymore. I staggered up and he managed somehow to come after me, weaving and stumbling and falling. I pushed him away.

"Go home, Lint. Go 'way."

The phone rang. We both stopped, bloody statues weaving in the wind.

"Bobbie!" Lint said through his blood.

It was Gloria, Obie's girl, calling to tell me that Obie had shot himself with the little .25 he'd given her for protection. He'd showed it to me once in college—a Japanese gun.

"Bobbie!" Lint shouted stupidly as he rushed for the phone.

And I hit him, him and his goddam Bobbie. He sank to the floor, not out, but unable to move. I'd left the phone dangling and now I hung up and rushed to throw water on my face and put on a jacket. I took a final look at Lint.

"Get the hell out before I get back," I told him. "This is my week for throwing all of you the hell out of my place. And you're getting your goddam Rocket job back too."

He began to struggle up and, to make sure he understood me, I kicked him one more time—a big one more—and then I rushed out as the neighbors were running to my apartment to see what the hell the noise was about.

I met Gloria in the hall of the hospital. "Was Obie staying with you?" I asked.

"No, he didn't want to. I didn't know where he was staying. He had been to my apartment. I found him in the hall with the gun and—and blood all over."

I went to emergency O.R. I wondered why they weren't operating. Obie lay on a stretcher in the "ready" room. A big pad was thrust up between the sheet and his chest. The rubber lines from blood plasma were taped to his arm. An oxygen tent stood near-by. The lines of Obie's face were deep and sharp; the color was gone. It was just gray. I felt somehow it was me lying there, but it seemed right for me to joke and say, "Man, get up from there—you owe me some lunch."

I could have sworn he smiled, that his lips formed the word. "Clown," but I couldn't be sure.

They rolled him inside, then, but made no move to begin an operation. An intern wearing dark-rimmed glasses came out with a cop.

"You his brother?" the cop asked. He looked at my beaten face quizzically as I thought, here we go again. All Negroes look alike.

"No. Friend."

"Any family?"

"Not in town," Gloria said. "I'm his—we were going to get married."

"I'm sorry," the intern said. "He lost too much blood. There's not much more we can do for him. The plasma isn't helping."

The cop stepped up again, pencil and pad ready. "Why did he do it?" he asked Gloria.

A humanitarian, I thought. No, a statistician. Gloria began to cry and turned away from him.

The cop looked at me. "You know?"

"I think so."

"Well?"

A young cop. A wife and kids and lives in Queens, I thought. "Got time to hear it?"

He looked at the intern. "I gotta have it for my report," he said, looking hard at me.

"Never mind," I said. How can you explain? "You wouldn't understand."

"What do you mean, 'Never mind'? Buddy, I told you I gotta have it."

"Not so loud," the intern said.

"Now," said the cop, "was he sick?"

"No."

"Money troubles?"

"No."

The cop lowered his voice so Gloria wouldn't hear him. "Woman trouble? Knock somebody up?"

"No."

The cop's mouth tightened into a thin line. "Depressed?"

"Sort of."

"Look, Johnny," the cop said with some exasperation, "I'm trying to help out."

"Thanks. The name's Mr. Hill, not Johnny."

He closed his pad with a snap.

I said, "I want to tell you why, but I can't in one word. I can't tell you in many words, and goddamit, I can't tell you at all unless you know and it's impossible for *you* to know why he did it."

"Forget it, Johnny," the cop said, walking away. "Just another dead nigger, that's all."

The intern followed him. I took Gloria out and put her in a cab. I didn't want to go with her. I didn't want anyone around to see me cry. I started walking through Central Park. The wind whipped the tears from my eyes. I cursed and damned into the wind. I wished I could squirm out of my skin, leave it to wither on the ground in the dark and grow a new one, like a snake.

Maybe I could run out of it. I tried. I raced through the park, head up, snatching breaths of air, and the only thing that happened was that I saw the moon. It was high and white in the sky, and the naked black limbs of the trees stretched gnarled, dun fingers toward it, as if to rip it from its place.

Lint was gone when I got home and it was a good thing, a damned good thing. I got drunk and I snotted and sniffled around quietly for one minute and screamed the next until the neighbors began pounding on the walls. They'd had enough from my place in one night to last them the next ten years. When I finally went to sleep I dreamed a large roach materialized out of the closet. It had Rollie's face. It scooted along the wall, then down to the floor. I was filled with revulsion as it came toward me, lights glistening on its back. It kept coming and coming, and I couldn't get out of the way. I trembled and collapsed with a groan just as it was about to touch me.

Early in the morning, while it was still gray, I woke and thought of my future. I had to quit Rocket that morning in order to pay off my debt to Lint, and that left me with nothing else at the moment— probably for a helluva lot of moments. Maybe, I thought, it wouldn't hurt to stay at Rocket for just one more week. I rubbed my eyes, then, and started to swing out of bed.

My legs wouldn't move.

I thought perhaps my muscles were stiff from the fighting and running the night before. I rubbed them some more, but I still couldn't get them to move. I became a little afraid and I started sobbing hoarsely. There was no one to help me, so I lay there calmly thinking, *I must quit Rocket and I must do it today.* For some reason I had connected my immobile legs with Rocket. I kept repeating it and soon I was able to move. I lighted a cigarette and thought about it. Yes, I would quit. What the hell was I thinking of, a compromise for a lousy week's salary?

I showered and felt better. I dressed slowly and carefully, and took the bus to the office. I saw I'd be late, but it didn't matter; I would never again be late for Rocket. I waited for a light to change at Fifth and 42nd and my legs seemed to go stiff on me again, but I murmured, "I'm going in to quit," and they seemed to be all right. The light changed and I crossed the street quickly, looking behind me at the Empire State Building, almost obscured by mist. I thought of Harriet then.

"Little late," the elevator operator observed.

"Yeah," I said.

"He looked at me, then turned back to the front of the car.

Sarah looked up when I walked in, but she said nothing. Leah gave me the big what's-the-matter-look and I winked at her. I draped my coat over my arm and walked into Rollie's office, closing the door behind me. He looked up and smiled pleasantly.

"How are you, Steve?"

"All right."

He looked at the closed door and the coat over my arm and his smile faded. "What's wrong, Steve?"

"Rollie, I'm quitting."

He made a scoffing sound. "What will you do? Where will you go?"

I shrugged. "I don't know. Right now I've got to rest. I'm not going to worry about anything else."

"Few problems outside the office?"

"Some problems in the office too, Rollie, as *you* know." The bastard tried to blush.

"Suppose," he said, "we give you that raise as of now?"

The offer shook me. "The bill a week?"

"Yes."

"No damned strings attached?"

"No strings," he said, blushing again.

"Haven't you been interviewing people for my job?"

"Yes, but I've decided none of them would work out."

"If I hadn't come in here this morning, you'd have let me continue working at my miserable salary?"

"I'm a business man, Steve."

"You're a damned fairy, Rollie—that's your business."

"Let's get back to the raise. It would be effective as of the first of the week."

I shook my head. "At one time it was the money, but not now, Rollie. I've got to quit altogether."

171

"Jesus, have some consideration for us!" he shouted.

"Consideration!" I said. I couldn't believe I'd heard it right. "For you?"

"Didn't we take you in and—"

"What!" I shouted. I felt myself getting hot. "What did you do? You underpaid me, tried to have me buy my raise by jumping over the sofa with you, and generally took advantage of me. That's what you did. Now what do *you* think you did?"

He flashed his dazzling smile and looked anxiously toward the door. "Don't get upset, Steve. We like your work. Few flaws here and there, lately, but we'd like you to stay."

"Rollie, you're not trying to understand me. I'm quitting today. Now."

He snarled, "Without notice? With all the work piled up in your office?" He stood up and placed his hands on his hips. "For some time now, I've had the idea you disliked this business. What's the matter with it? Not good enough for you?"

He asked, I answered. "It stinks!"

He waved a soft hand. "There was a future in it for you."

"Not for me."

"Business grows every year."

"One year it'll explode. With things like Crispus happening, how long do you think you can continue to play with people's dreams, wrap them up in a pretty jacket? People die for dreams, Rollie." I laughed at him. "You screwed up Crispus and you almost died for his dream."

His face whitened.

I put on my coat. "Can I get my check now?"

"No," he shouted, slamming things down on his desk. "You'll have to come in next week."

"Mail it to me," I said, starting for the door.

He rushed from behind his desk. "Who do you think *you* are, pretending to have a conscience? Our money used to be good enough for you."

He was right, I could say nothing to that.

"You've got to live like the rest of us," he said. "You think it's going to be better anywhere else for you? Do you think *you're* going to find it easier?" His eyes became cold and he said softly, "You're Negro—some people would call you a nigger, but not me. You're Negro, and for you it's always going to be tough."

The fear set off by the truth of what he said charged through me. I leaped forward, fear and anger again boiling, and grabbed him by the lapels of his jacket. He merely stood there, making no move to defend himself. That, and the look on his face, threw me for a moment.

The rest happened quickly. I drew back—it seemed that lately I was always pulling back a fist; me, a guy who loves nothing more than working out a line of iambic pentameter—and started forward. I could feel hate pumping hotly through my arm and my brain tingled with anticipation of striking the blow. Here I was again, a mere twelve hours later in another stupid fight, but it had come to this; there would no longer be any compromise with the insults. As fast as they came, goddamit, that was as fast as I was going to try to handle them.

I could hear the sound of my fist landing against his jaw. I could see him flying back into the wall, see the blood spring like a new well from his mouth. And my arm was coming forward again. I exulted in the clean way it plunged away from my shoulder. Lint, the evening before, had been for me and me alone, but this would be for Teddy and Frankie and all the kids like them who might have to face Rollies on the way up. And it would be for the little old ladies upstate and in Minnesota who sank their money in Rocket books.

And then, clumsily and with much scraping of the feet, I stopped. I stood trembling, looking at Rollie, who with wide eyes moved away.

There he was, half-man, half-woman, typical of our stop-go, no-yes, hello-good-bye world; split. He had been ready to stand there and feed on my violence, to let it do something which could make his world and personality whole. That's what their massive retaliation was, Obie, the plugging up of their world rent with holes through which people like Crispus and Rollie climbed at the same time from opposite sides.

I had it, Obie, I had it. Let them shake and expect the violence they deserve, but never, never give it to them, Obie, because they derive strength from it, as Rollie wanted strength from me now. But I wasn't going to give it to him.

I waved good-bye to Rollie and left his office. I saluted Leah on the way out. I stopped at the cigarette counter downstairs. I was out of smokes and needed a lift badly. My eyes sought out the English Ovals, the cigarettes I smoked when I was flush. I thought of the lean days ahead and considered whether I should spend the extra pennies for the Ovals, or stick to my regular brand, five cents less.

"To hell with it," I said aloud.

"Sir?" the clerk said.

"Ovals."

He gave me the pack, then the matches. I paid him and hurried into the street. I hopped aboard a bus. I wanted to get home quickly.

I rushed into the apartment and picked up the phone, wondering what my folks would say when I told them in my next letter. I dialed her number and waited while I got transferred from one extension to another.

Finally she was on, saying breathlessly, "Steve! Steve! What is it? What's happened?"

"Nothing, baby, nothing. Sorry to call you at work. Listen, I've been sort of out of my mind for a while, but now I got some sense and I wonder if you'd marry me in a few months or so. I have to get another job—it has to be a good one because I don't want to live in Albany and I—"

"Yes."

"What did you say?"

"I said yes. What did you think I was going to say?"

"Grace, I don't know. People have been saying so damned many things lately."

"Are you all right?"

"Never better."

"Shall I come down this week end?"

"No. I want to come up."

Cautiously, she asked, "Are you sober?"

"Yes. You don't think I'd ask you to marry me if I were drunk, do you? I ask everyone else when I'm drunk."

Her laughter came bubbling out of the phone and I laughed too, I swear to God. For the first time in centuries, it seemed, I laughed.

"C'mon, get off," I said. "You're running up the bill. Have to watch that."

"See you Friday."

She was gone then. I rushed to put the coffee on and got on the phone again.

"Mr. Graff, please," I said. I hummed as I waited.

"Hello, Steve! How are you?"

"You remember me?"

"Did you think I'd forgotten you?"

"Well, I didn't know."

"Glad you called. Got time to talk about some things?"

"Right now," I said, as the coffee began to perk merrily on the gas, "I've a few minutes. I'll see you in an hour, if that's all right."

"That's fine. See you then."

I stood up as I sipped my coffee and peered out the window. It seemed that spring was coming early.